The Narrow Road

A Pilgrim's Progress

The Narrow Road

A Pilgrim's Progress

By Erik Yeager
Illustrated by David DelaGardelle

Edited by Howard Allen

Based on
The Pilgrim's Progress
By John Bunyan

The Narrow Road Film Company, LLC
2013

First Printing: 2013

ISBN 978-0-9912645-1-3

The Narrow Road Film Company, LLC
Tucson, Arizona
info@narrowroadmovie.com

www.narrowroadmovie.com

To John Bunyan and so many others who have suffered for their faith,

With special thanks to our Kickstarter supporters.

PROLOGUE

John's heart sank as he heard his monstrous jailer, Despair, approaching the ancient oak door that held him captive for nearly as long as he could remember. Through cracks in the door, dim light flickered into John's dungeon cell from hall torches as John pressed himself flat against the carved stone wall where he awaited his next intrusion underneath an inscription from days past, the meaning of which John could never seem to remember:

JOHN FELL INTO A HOLE.

IN THAT HOLE JOHN DREAMED A DREAM.

The iron latch creaked downward and the door opened. John dared to move only his eyes to see what his captor intended with him. It wasn't mealtime, which always meant trouble. As the giant Ogre came into view, John saw that Despair was dragging a lifeless human form behind him. When he reached the center of the cell, Despair carelessly dropped his load and turned back to the door.

Despair paused just before exiting and smiled widely enough for all his cracked and crooked teeth to be revealed in the torchlight that was now brighter through the open door.

"Brought you a friend," Despair sneered, followed by a terrible roar of sick delight. He slammed the door shut and locked it before lumbering away, as loudly as ever. John squeezed his eyes shut as the Ogre's laughter echoed down the corridor.

When he was sure Despair was quite out of range, John leapt from his place against the craggy wall and shouted on the edge of hysterics, more to himself than to his captor, "Friend? Friend? I can still smell the rotten stench from the last one!"

His eyes darted over to a dirt patch across the cell from where he stood as he remembered the last prisoner who was carried here; protruding from a makeshift grave were the face of a skull, the tips of several ribs, and the top half of a skeletal foot.

"Sorry mate, no offence intended," said John to the morbid space. "I'm sure I don't smell like roses, either."

John no longer had any idea how many years he had spent as a captive of Despair, the Ogre that terrorized this region of the Demon Lord Apollyon's realm from Doubting Castle. And yet Despair was merely vile next to Apollyon and the horror that was his centuries of lordship, aided by the hellish demon hordes under his control who scoured every inch of the Earth for human food to feed their insatiable, hate-filled appetites. It was bitter irony that John felt safer in the clutches of Despair's dungeon than out in the world enslaved to Apollyon and all those allied to him—be they demon or human. Though they weren't allies exactly, Apollyon seemed unconcerned with Despair, probably because of their shared distaste for humankind.

John barked out a short ragged laugh at this. And then another and another, so that any who heard him might conclude him to be a madman. There was little doubt in John's own mind that he was insane.

The sound of a breath not his own broke the reverie. John stared at the newcomer and held his breath for complete silence. After a moment, he was sure that he saw the movement of an inhaled breath where the man's bare neck met the top of his worn leather breastplate. John scrambled on hands and knees to the man and placed an ear on his leather-covered chest. It was nearly inaudible, but through the layers John could hear the faintest of *thump-thumps*.

"You're alive!" John folded himself over backwards and faced the ceiling. "My God...!" John was surprised that word, that *name*, was uttered from his lips and his mind swam with images of the dark prison environment that he believed had destroyed any remaining thought of God, or El Shaddai, as He was commonly called.

John returned his thoughts to his new "friend". You are alive, my friend, he thought, but I do not think you will find this life such a great fortune when you awake.

Soon after, John had the man's body pulled against a wall—the most unlikely place to be trampled by Despair—where he did his best to clean the man's face and surface wounds from the bowl of dirty water he collected from a drip above. The man was built well, certainly difficult to move in battle, and with a face shaped and set like a well-chiseled sculpture. It was imperative that John get this man to consciousness. John had forgotten the isolation that came with his situation, but now the presence of another living soul brought back the torturing pangs of his drawn-out loneliness.

A *clang* from the outside startled John. He froze all movement and breath, listening for any hint that Despair was returning to the cell. Another *clang* threw John's gaze to the door, but no steps could be heard nor the deep grunting that usually accompanied them. As John turned his attention back to the man he caught sight of an object on the floor nearby where the man had been dropped. He checked the man once, saw his eyes tightly closed, and then made his way to the object.

There, spattered with dry blood and bound in tattered and worn leather, was a book. John quickly opened it and began to read.

CHAPTER ONE

SIX MONTHS EARLIER

Christian raised high his goblet of wine.

"To my young friend's last meal as a free man!" he declared to the small audience of family and neighbors gathered around the outdoor dining table.

A chorus of "Hear, hear!" and "Cheers!" and "Aye!" sang back to him, and to Faithful—the young man to whom the toast had been directed.

"My boy, your father would be so proud," said Deedee, Faithful's mother. She then looked at Christian and her smiling face became serious. "And you take care of him, Christian. You will find no better companion in your duties."

Christian nodded. "Try not to worry. The wilderness of this world has many ways of bonding men as friends...as brothers. We will look after each other." He looked at Faithful, who had resumed a faux duel with Christian's eldest son, Matthew. "I see his maturity each time I return home. He will be alright."

Comforted by his words, Deedee returned her gaze to the table and to the meal before her. Christian smiled and spread his arms wide, encompassing the whole dining table. At this signal, everyone commenced serving themselves from the feast that Deedee and Christy, Christian's wife, had prepared to celebrate Faithful's first assignment as Christian's assistant the following morning.

Christian was anxious about leaving his family again for another assignment and found it difficult to enjoy the celebration. He did his best to hide his anxiety from his family and guests, and most of all Faithful, and yet it was somehow fitting that it was all unfolding beneath the weeping willow tree that stood off to the side of Christian's modest whitewashed wattle and daub cottage of oak framework. Christian felt that the willow was the only piece of nature that shared

5

his sadness and how every fiber of his being bent beneath the burden of his duties as a Tracer with each new assignment.

The tree marked the beginning of a sizable tract of serene farmland. Christian's family, and Faithful's, lived on the outskirts of Destruction with twenty or thirty other similar farm cottages scattered around the southern outskirts of the bustling city. Their property was the sort that was desired by many of the thousands of urban folk, who mostly lived in leaning rows of timber-frame dwellings stacked one on top of the other, often three levels high. Christian was fortunate to have such a beautiful property and a home of rare privacy, obtained in large part due to his famous work as a Tracer, or man tracker.

Christy caught his eye and he knew that now was not the time for this kind of introspection. Faithful could not be allowed to detect any hint of reservation or gloom the night before both men were to set out on their first assignment together.

* * *

When the dinner had ended, Christian wandered into the kitchen with a tower of plates and goblets. He set them down where he was directed to by Deedee and then entered the family room, closed the door behind him for privacy, and took a seat at his large desk. After a moment of staring blankly at the set of locked doors in the small box cabinet, Christian drew a collection of keys from under his shirt, which hung from a thin silver chain around his neck. He selected the appropriate key, inserted it into one of the doors, and turned it with a *click*. Inside were various important documents, a locked chest, and a shrouded object that had the form of a large, misshapen skull. Christian drew a deep breath and nearly became entranced by the object, save for the gentle knock on the door leading to the room. It was Christy.

"Come in," said Christian. "And please shut the door behind you," he added once she was in the room. When she had done so she crossed the room and stood behind her seated husband, then lovingly placed her hands on his shoulders.

"I have seen you anxious before, my love, and you know that I always dread your departure, but never before now have I feared that you might *not* leave your home."

Christian placed the shrouded object on the floor and closed and locked the cabinet once more, and then he looked at his wife. Seeing the concern in her eyes was almost more than he could endure at such a vulnerable moment.

"Each journey is more difficult than the last," he finally said when he was sure that his voice would not break.

"You *are* still going on patrol in the morning," Christy checked.

As if hearing her inquiry and expecting a wrong answer from Christian, the volcanic peak of Mount Apollyon outside the windows flared to life belching black smoke and lava that disappeared against the twilight.

"Of course I am going." Christian kept his eyes on the great mountain just beyond Destruction to the north. Terrible images and the screams of men and women in ragged dark brown cowls entered his mind.

Christian knew that if Christy truly understood the work he did—the terrible things he was forced to do in order to protect and provide for his family—she would be less concerned with her own well-being than for that of the poor souls who came across Christian and his demon overlords in the wilderness. Empathy was one of the traits Christian admired most in his wife, and it was because of this quality that she could never know the full truth about his work. Christian had long ago decided that he would carry this heavy burden alone.

When what little he did share would not explain his night terrors, Christian resorted to describing some of the horrible sights he had seen but not participated in, such as the horrors of the once-great town of Mansoul, or events from the Great Rebellion that he participated in so long ago, during his youth. He never discussed his present work.

"The last campaign took me closer to the edges of Mansoul than I expected. That town is nothing like the idyllic sanctuary we visited toward the end of our courtship. The shadow of Apollyon's mountain is always upon it now. The most dangerous rebels are...*questioned* there...before meeting their terrible fates within the fiery depths of Mount Apollyon itself."

Christy placed a reassuring hand on her husband's knee.

"They know as well as we that resistance against King Apollyon is futile. They have made their choice and must suffer the consequences, as dreadful as they may be," she replied in a comforting tone that was sincere but misinformed. Christian knew that few residents of Destruction truly understood their enemies. Christian, who had himself been on the front lines of this endless battle for most of his adult life, hardly understood the enemy. But for his part, Christian's ignorance was a defense mechanism allowing him to endure his days of service. "And you have made *your* choice to protect your family and your home—as well as your fellow citizens here in Destruction—at all costs."

Christian knew that his wife was merely trying to comfort him, but he also feared that if she ever became aware of the true cost of serving Apollyon, she would not feel so loyal to him or so secure in her "safe" life in Destruction. Bearing this burden alone was sometimes as difficult as doing the work itself, but Christian believed that any attempt at confessing his sins to his wife would be purely selfish and serve no purpose other than lightening the burden his own guilt. He was also afraid of how Christy would feel about him if she knew the kind of soldier he truly was. How could she not hate him if she knew?

Christy had rarely seen any measure of the terrible sights that haunted Christian's dreams. They had known only one family from their city who had chosen to side with the rebellion against Apollyon. Not only was the family never heard from again, but their house and land had been torched along with six of the surrounding cottages for good measure. It had been a hellish night that Christian knew his wife would never forget, nor could he. Despite the years since, he still imagined that the soot from the fires covered his body no matter how often he washed. King Apollyon tolerated no opposition and believed wholly in the power of random acts of cruelty and terror to quell any thoughts of rebellion. It was a ruthless strategy that seemed to bear results given Destruction's long history of requiring no standing detachments of soldiers from Apollyon's nearby regiments, and also providing some of the best Tracers (man-hunters like Christian) for his scouting parties. However, Christian doubted that Christy believed her husband capable of enforcing such draconian orders.

9

"Well," said Christian finally, "I had better get this helmet to Faithful so that he can get used to its weight."

Christy smiled. "He is out in the stables."

Christian stood to leave as his wife placed a gentle hand on his arm and smiled with a smile that Christian knew held back the sorrow she surely felt at her husband's nearing departure.

"Don't forget that Sammie and Matthew will want to spend time with their father before he leaves at dawn," she managed.

Christian added his own brave smile to hers at the mention of their children. They had seen so little of life and of their father, and he so little of them.

"I can think of no better way to spend my last hours at home."

There was a door that led from the family room, around the back of the cottage to the barn where the small horse stable was located. Upon entering, Christian found Faithful gazing out a thin opening in the wall that provided fresh air to the solitary horse. The opening happened to face Mount Apollyon, the peak on the horizon that caught Faithful's attention. The young man made no indication that he could hear the clatter of dishes being cleaned after the party in his honor. Christian made sure not to shuffle his feet as a way of testing the passive awareness of his newly-promoted assistant. Faithful had previously served as a foot soldier and must have shown great endurance and promise as a tracker in order to be recommended as a Tracer.

When Christian was nearly six paces away Faithful said, "Will you ever quit testing me?"

Christian smiled, then replied, "We will find every opportunity to hone our skills and keep our senses alert." He then extended his arm with the hand that clasped the heavy hidden object. "Here. This is yours now."

Faithful turned to Christian and looked at the strange gift that was being offered to him. Christian nodded his head, confirming to Faithful that the item was indeed his to take. Faithful took it and removed the pale cloth covering. Staring back at him was a newly crafted steel helmet. Across the front was a faceplate that looked something like a skull complete with hollowed-out eyes for the wearer to see through and slits over the nose and a mouth (likely more for effect than for the wearer to breathe through).

"I hope it fits," said Faithful, turning the helmet around to view the back.

"It will fit well enough," Christian replied. He turned to his horse, a large mount of rich black color and white spots, and began to stroke the creature's neck above the withers.

"How do you spot a demon?"

"As a Tracer," Faithful replied in confusion, "won't it be my job to track people?"

Christian gazed at him for a moment but did not repeat the question. The young man still needed to learn how to think critically about every detail and scenario, no matter how mundane they might seem.

"Well, you can see them of course," Faithful finally answered, though he sounded like he knew he was giving an insufficient answer.

"By then it's too late. You need to sense them before you see them. Do you recall the poem?"

"In my sleep. How can I forget it the way you drilled it into me: 'Bitter cold and dark, death's stench and sulfur, bitter cold and dark, daytime slumber.'"

"What does that mean?" Christian pressed.

"Well...demons stink. And the air gets colder and darker in their presence. But why does that matter if we are on their side?"

Christian stood back and looked out the barn door to make sure he wouldn't be overheard. He could not risk exposing the great secret of his work as a Tracer to his family, who along with most other residents of Destruction believed Tracers to be human fugitive trackers who would find Apollyon's enemies hiding in the wilderness and hand them over to demonkind for interrogation, imprisonment, and then possibly "just" execution for treason.

"You need to think like our enemy, Faithful," said Christian in a low voice. "We know how to spot demons, and therefore to evade them if we wish. So might Evangelists. Our alliance with demonkind works because the demons will leave us—and our families—alone if we find them food elsewhere." Christian watched

11

Faithful for a moment. He seemed to struggle with this notion so Christian felt it best to hammer the point home. "We find their next meal, or we become it."

Faithful remained deep in thought for some time, and Christian decided it best to allow the young man some time to process what had been said. It was several minutes before Faithful finally spoke again, in a low voice.

"Are our lives worth so much more than theirs?"

Christian set his face in a stern manner. "Worth more to whom?"

Faithful looked down at the helmet in his hands, considering Christian's response. Christian reminded himself that he could not blame his companion for asking a question that he had asked himself many times before. The laughter of his children interjected from the yard into the barn, making the situation even more difficult to address objectively. Christian thought back to the fires that had consumed seven of Destruction's most coveted homes—families that had paid the price for someone else's treason; good folk who had not been given an opportunity to prove their fealty to their lord. Could he really believe that he was somehow better than any of them? "We're just luckier, I suppose. Or perhaps smarter."

Faithful quickly moved his eyes up to Christian's, and then over Christian's shoulder.

"It looks like my mother is ready to head home." He paused, waiting to see if Christian had any further counsel. He did not, as he was already pondering how best to expend his energy so that sleep would come quickly tonight.

"I'd better be off then," Faithful continued. "Big day tomorrow."

Faithful turned to leave and then remembered one final thought. "Oh, thanks for the party," he added with a smile.

Christian smiled back and then held Faithful's gaze. The young man did not flinch. This was good.

"Sunrise. Don't be late."

After Faithful had departed and Christian spent some time tending to his beloved farm horse, he joined his family inside for an evening of conversation and games. When Christian finally retired to bed, sleep indeed came fast, and with it dreams of consuming fire, tortured screams, and feasting demons.

CHAPTER TWO

Christian emerged from his cottage and found that the weather reflected his mood: blue-grey, foggy, and heavy-laden. In the light of the rising sun, he saw the wooden play-sword belonging to his son Matthew lying carelessly in the grass, forgotten after last night's festivities. Christian moved to the place where it lay, picked it up, and rested it against the outside wall of the family's house—right next to his own travelling pack and real blade that curved slightly toward the tip.

Faithful soon emerged from the morning mist with his travelling pack slung over a shoulder and his sheathed sword in hand. Faithful wore the same steel armor as Christian, except for two differences: it was fresh from the forge and therefore contained none of the permanent scratches and dents that Christian's had earned, also the leather breastplate of Faithful's armor was barren except for a miniature relief of an Apollyon demon-head over the sternum, whereas Christian's depicted the same emblem across the entire chest in a manner that gave the appearance of a branding and caused the lighter areas to reflect the moonlight for an added supernatural effect. Otherwise the armor of both men included triple-layered steel shoulder pauldrons that extended down to just above the elbow, steel vambraces covering the top of each forearm, hardened-leather faulds that hung from the plackart over the front of both hips, and steel greaves that covered their lower legs down to the ankle. The armor was intended to be light enough for Tracers to engage in tracking and pursuit, and heavy enough to prevent most common forms of attack.

"Good morning!" said Faithful the moment he arrived beside Christian, who responded with only the briefest wave of a hand. He bent down to retrieve two long chains and indicated for Faithful to turn his back to him and remove the pack from his shoulder.

"Did you say goodbye to your mother?" Christian asked as he took Faithful's sheathed sword and wove each of the chains through one of two broad loops on the back of the sheath.

"Barely. I could hardly get a word in edge-wise. She's so proud that her..." Faithful changed the tone of his voice to mimic that of his mother "'...baby boy will fulfill the family vow and pay the blood-price for her freedom and security. And learn from a legendary Tracer, no less!' You'd think I'd never been on the front lines before."

Christian chuckled as he crisscrossed the chains across his companion's torso and hooked each end into one of the links so that they were snug but not overly uncomfortable, though in fact the very purpose of the chains was to be an ever-present reminder to the Tracers of their inescapable service to Apollyon.

"She said that about a dozen times," Faithful added.

Christian was really in no mood for small talk. "Better to be the hunter than the hunted."

"The whole city says you're the best."

Christian silently picked up Faithful's pack, unhooked the strap, fed the strip of canvas behind the sword sheath, and refastened it again so that the pack lay atop the sword sheath while also keeping it just off the handle for easy accessibility.

"Won't the pack get in the way when I draw my sword?" There was some concern in Faithful's voice.

"Not if you ordered your pack correctly," Christian replied. He turned Faithful so that the men were facing each other. "There." Christian indicated his own pack and blade. "Now do the same for me."

Faithful drew his sword partially out of its sheath and smirked with satisfaction as he re-sheathed it. He then completed the task of Christian's pack in silence, magnifying the sound of the clinking chains. Faithful's shaking hands told Christian that reality was beginning to set in for the young man.

Suddenly Faithful pumped a fist into the air and declared, "To hunting!" Christian held back a rebuke, deciding that it was just Faithful's way of dealing with his nerves. He would be fine once they got started.

The arrival of Christy's beautiful face at the door indicated that Faithful's pronouncement of nervous courage had drawn the attention of Christian's household. Christy came out of the cottage with Joseph asleep on her shoulder and Matthew and Sammie clinging to her sleeping gown. She held Christian's helmet in her hand.

"I thought you might need this," she said before smiling wearily.

"What would I do without you?" asked Christian, adding his own half-hearted grin to hers. Christian's smiled faded quickly as he considered the question and inwardly reacted to the sobering answer that came to mind: he could not survive without Christy, and his family would be in great peril without him. He could see that Christy, too, must be having similar thoughts. Though her smile did not fade, he could see the fear in her eyes that was typical at his departures.

Christian finally knelt on a knee to face his son and daughter, and both took turns embracing him.

"Be good," Christian said to them.

"We will," they answered in sleepy voices.

"Listen to your mother," he added.

"We will," came their responses, nearly in unison. Christian held his gaze upon his eldest son.

"I *will!*" came the annoyed confirmation from Matthew.

Christian smiled and nodded, satisfied, and stood back up to face his wife. He kissed his still-sleeping baby boy, Joseph, on the forehead, and then planted a firm kiss on Christy embracing her tightly.

After he released her he placed a hand on the helmet, but Christy maintained her tight grip on it with his own.

"You do what must be done," she urged and again Christian thought of how differently she would feel about him if she *really* knew what must be done. Would she still love him? Could she? "Keep us safe," she continued. "Think of nothing else."

Christian nodded, "Always."

She released her grip on the helmet and as Christian placed it on his head he could not help but notice his children retreating behind Christy's legs, hardly daring to peek out. He lingered on this image for longer than he should have, and then forced himself to look at Faithful. With a nod his new companion donned his helmet as well, and then both Tracers turned and started up the road. Neither looked back.

CHAPTER THREE

The first days of their journey took Christian and Faithful toward their assigned patrol route. The men's homes in the Outskirts were far to the north of their present location, and northward still were Destruction and Mount Apollyon. To their more-immediate south was the packed city of Recanto, where Christy had grown up, which had grown considerably under Apollyon's reign and was one of the bulwarks of his rule in this part of the world. There seemed to be little danger of the Evangelist Rebellion ever permeating Apollyon's control over the region. In fact, Recanto had swelled to the point that many like Christy's family were moving from Recanto to Destruction, though historically people preferred to avoid living in Destruction's close proximity to Mount Apollyon.

The real hot beds of sedition, Christian had explained to Faithful, were towns further to the east near Vanity, Apollyon's easternmost fortress city, and beyond. Apollyon's armies were stationed in force in towns and cities across the east and therefore Tracers were less necessary because armies could round up "food" in greater quantities. Christian suspected that there was no way of hiding this horrifying truth from the residents of those eastern cities and he wondered how the masses dealt with such open evil in their midst.

Tracers, like Christian and Faithful, were more useful in the wilderness areas where the enemy so often hid out after fleeing from Apollyon's larger forces while attempting to infiltrate Apollyon's inner cities. The Evangelists' goal was to blend in and spread their message of dissension and rebellion.

"Our assignment will have us patrolling the woods between Recanto and Temporal City, which is southeast of Recanto," said Christian. "There is a dense wood surrounding that city and Evangelists like to lay their ideological ambushes

there upon the unsuspecting traveler. We will stick mostly to the woods through-
out our assignment, and will likely be joined by our demon counterparts in a few
days' time."

Faithful was silent for a long while, taking in the information Christian had
given him and, no doubt, picturing what all these towns, cities, and regions
looked like. Finally, he rubbed the stubble that had grown on his face.

"I was told that you had been to Mansoul on your last assignment. I've heard
rumors that it is very different from how it used to be. I used to visit there with
my father when I was very young, though I haven't been back since he died all
those years ago. I know a place never stays exactly the same, but has it changed
so much?"

"Mansoul is far to the north—east of Destruction—and far outside of our
charge."

"I know that," Faithful replied. "I'm only curious."

Christian did not look at Faithful. Mansoul was his least favorite topic and
he had hoped to avoid discussing the nightmare-town. It was difficult enough to
get the horrible images out of his head without dredging up painful memories for
the sake of conversation. Furthermore, he had no desire to spoil his friend's cher-
ished childhood memories.

"There are many rumors floating around Destruction about Mansoul. You
shouldn't believe everything you hear."

"I've heard it is a mere shadow of the place I remember so fondly," Faithful
continued, anxiously.

"Quite literally, actually, now that Mansoul lies under the shadow of Mount
Apollyon's cloud."

Faithful remained silent, expecting Christian to continue. Christian needed
Faithful to be focused on their assignment and after a moment of silent thought
he realized that, despite the discomfort, sobering him up might be the best way
to impart the seriousness of their charge, so the veteran Tracer begrudgingly re-
lated to his assistant every gruesome detail to which he had been witness
concerning the present situation of Mansoul, including the foul tortures on the

boldest insurgents by demons and how the Evangelists and rebel captains were given over to the most depraved of Apollyon's servants.

"Mansoul is now a forlorn collection of knotted hovels and prisons, and its once-great citadel at the far edge of the city has been allowed to fall into sordid disrepair by the hellish monsters and demonkind that now occupy its courts and chambers. The incessant moans and pleas for mercy in that place would surely drive to insanity any man who tarried outside the high enclosing walls."

The only facts Christian withheld from Faithful were the prisons stuffed with women and children, and the talk of the unique horrors visited upon them there. These images haunted Christian nearly every night since his return to Destruction and gave rise to a recurring nightmare of his family's torment and gruesome destruction at the hands of demonic forces—a nightmare so dramatic that Christian swore it was more akin to a vision due to the fact that he could recall its graphic nature long after he had awoken. In fact, the nightmare's imagery often occupied his waking thoughts.

By the time Christian finished recounting his most recent encounter with Mansoul, dusk was upon the Tracers and Faithful looked pale in the fading light. The younger man was at a loss for words.

"As long as we are diligent in our duties," Christian added, "we will have nothing to fear." It was probably a lie, but Faithful would be better to hear it. "The sooner Apollyon turns his attention to Yeshua in the Far East the sooner Destruction will be out from the darkest parts of his shadow." Perhaps that last statement was a lie too, but it was all Christian had to placate his raging mind.

"What do you know about Yeshua?" Faithful finally asked.

"Just what everyone knows, I guess," Christian replied.

Faithful looked curiously at Christian, and so Christian continued, "Yeshua is said to be the King of Celestial City in the east—further east than the hill country of Beulah—and Son of the Evangelists' God, El Shaddai. The Evangelists worship Yeshua and claim to be doing His work. They also claim that He is immortal—resurrected from the dead by His own power. At least I believe that is the myth."

"Is there more to the myth?"

"Probably," Christian replied, "but there is a limit to what I hear on patrol and Yeshua is a forbidden topic among demonkind."

"And where is Beulah?"

"Beulah lies to the east of Vanity and it is said to be quite beautiful. I have never been there myself, but El Shaddai's city is rumored to be just east of Beulah across a great river."

"You seem to know a good deal more about Yeshua than anyone else I've spoken with," said Faithful.

"Then I've said too much," Christian joked with the uncomfortable realization that he had, in fact, said too much. "I have been around a long time and have seen and heard more than my fair share of talk about the rebellion, but talk of Yeshua is dangerous. I have lost many friends to rebellion and I don't care to lose any more."

Faithful remained deep in thought for a long while. He finally broke the silence.

"Like my father?" Faithful asked. Christian's heart sank.

"Was my father one of the friends you lost…to rebellion?"

Christian remained silent for another long moment and took several deep breaths before answering. "Your father was a great friend and his death was tragic. I would not wish his fate upon you."

"Why doesn't Yeshua help His followers?" Faithful asked and Christian could detect a tone of anger. "Does He always remain so far from their cries?"

"To be honest, I'm not convinced that Yeshua even exists. At least, not anymore. Even if He does exist, why would He be any different than Apollyon? Evangelists boast that Yeshua is everywhere and yet it seems clear that He leaves His followers to fend for themselves. At least Apollyon makes himself seen to his people from time to time, not that the experience is all that enjoyable." He winked and let a grin curl up one side of his face.

Faithful let a low chuckle escape and Christian saw that some color was finally returning to his cheeks as Faithful continued to look straight ahead. "So how do you know that Yeshua is no different than King Apollyon? I mean, why would Apollyon need an army, or Tracers, if Yeshua and His supporters were so few in number or unthreatening?"

"I'm afraid I can offer you no real answers," Christian replied candidly. "I can only pass along rumors, and what good is that? The truth is that *our* concern is the service of Apollyon and his demon brethren. They should be your focus."

Faithful glanced at him. "It's just that... I would just like to hear one of these Evangelists with my own ears. If what they have to say is so wrong then our lord should not be afraid—"

Christian planted a firm palm against his companion's shoulder, stopping them both in their tracks. The momentum turned Faithful so that he was partly facing Christian. "You should be more careful with your words. We are not as alone on this road as you might presume, especially with night fast approaching. Demons will not tolerate talk of insurrection." Christian thought a moment more and then added, "Now is not the time to chase ghosts from our past."

Faithful cast his eyes to the ground. "I'm sorry, sir."

Both men allowed the still night air to pass between them for several breaths. Then Faithful said, "I want to be sure that we are fighting on the right side, Christian. You would know this better than anyone."

"What is that supposed to mean?" Christian replied, and with more harshness than he intended.

"Nothing! I just figured with your years of experience, and that you have never proven false to me, that you would know as much as anyone."

Christian looked at Faithful with hard eyes, wondering how long Faithful had been harboring these doubts. He realized that he was still holding firmly to Faithful's shoulder and removed his hand.

Christian moved his hand to his face, rubbing his own salt-and-pepper shadow of a beard. He studied Faithful long enough that the younger man became shifty with his eyes and began to toe at the dirt around his feet. Faithful was right, after all. The vague excuses that Christian now hurled at Faithful were never enough to fully appease Christian's own doubts. In fact, Christian was once part of a Great Rebellion—though it was not led by Yeshua's followers nor even for His cause—which had born too great a cost. The truth was that Christian *needed*

21

to believe that these wide-spread assumptions about Yeshua and his misguided followers had merit, or he might not have the strength to continue fighting an "enemy" that he, in reality, knew so little about in the service of a demon king he had once so vehemently rebelled against.

"You are right," Christian said finally. "I should know more, but the Evangelists still remain a mystery to me. I know from experience that these Evangelists would be martyrs and do not think twice about bringing others to death with them, others who may not be so willing. I also know that to turn against Apollyon would mean certain death for my family, and that is a price I cannot pay."

Christian indicated that the men should continue walking, and then he continued to speak.

"These usurpers make rebellion against Apollyon and romanticize their actions to catch itching ears and beating hearts like yours, Faithful. To me, it all sounds like the fairytale imaginings of people who seek escape from the harsh reality of this world: Apollyon is undefeatable. The plain reality, Faithful, is that we are on the side that best allows us to control our own fates. You can declare that we are all pawns of two opposing forces greater than ourselves, and I would agree. But only *one* side has clearly provided us the opportunity to protect those who we love in this life from troublemakers who bring nothing but death and division wherever they go."

It took several moments, but finally Faithful nodded his head, which was the only response he could manage. His posture indicated that he had been drained of every ounce of hope for a life lived without Apollyon, and Christian believed that he had effectively communicated his warning.

"Okay." Christian's voice had quickly returned to a normal tone, more out of necessity than a feeling of calm. "We are expected to begin Tracing tomorrow. Let us set up camp here for the night and get started at first light."

Within a half hour the camp was in order and both men were on their blankets beside a low-smoldering fire, fighting restless thoughts and willing sleep to finally come.

                                          *   *   *

Christian pressed his finger across his lips to signal silence. He then pointed to a small clearing below the cliff that he and Faithful were looking over. The late afternoon sunlight streamed through the tall trees and beams of all sizes painted bright patches wherever they landed on the forest floor, but none landed on the crude camp that four Evangelists had set up in the clearing. They likely thought that the tall cliff would afford their campfire some protection from night winds. Christian signaled for Faithful to draw back to the road.

"What now?" whispered Faithful as audibly as he dared once Christian had joined him.

"Judging by how careless they have been in setting up their camp, this group appears to be new to this conflict. Still, we will keep an eye on them until our superiors arrive, which should be a couple of hours yet."

Those last hours of day likely seemed an eternity for Faithful; at least they had for Christian on his first patrol. The Tracers sat about twenty paces from the cliff's edge with one of them checking on the Evangelists every ten minutes or so. Faithful had taken the final check and when he returned his walk was slow, and not because of the darkening sky. He swallowed roughly, giving Christian the impression that Faithful was nervous about his first face-to-face meeting with a demon. He'd be a fool not to be apprehensive, Christian thought.

"You will get accustomed well enough to their presence," said Christian. "Keep them focused on their appetites and they will hardly take notice of you."

"This all seems wrong—"

"Hey! It is not *our* fault that Yeshua's leaders provide such ill-training to their followers. You would think they would learn by now. Well, these few will get a cruel education tonight. Unfortunately they will not be able to pass along their experience, but perhaps their leaders will finally change their plans when they find their ranks thinned a bit more by morning."

Christian detected a fleeting hint of distaste turn up Faithful's upper lip at these words. "So that is how we justify this?" the young man said.

"You need to get your head right, boy! This is no time for philosophical debates." It was all Christian could do to keep his voice low. "*The Evangelists* are the enemy, they are the ones who provoke Apollyon's anger and make life more difficult for those of us living closest to his mountain, they are the ones who cannot live and let live, and *they* certainly cannot be counted on to defend you any more than you can rely on their precious far-away Yeshua! As long as they spread His poisonous false hope to our cities and towns you can bet that Apollyon will continue to make our lives miserable and there will be no end to these wretched assignments so far from home." Christian calmed himself with a deep breath. "I want to grow old with my family rather than being ripped away from them year after year to come out to this forsaken land to fill the bellies of demons who would just as soon feast on our flesh as that of the Evangelists'. I want this war far away from here and driving these rebels out is the only means to that end. Perhaps, when there is no more rebellion, Apollyon and his demon hordes will return to the depths of Mount Apollyon and leave mankind alone on the Earth."

Faithful was clearly confused, still knowing so little about demonkind. "Leave Earth? Then what would they eat?"

"Demons only need to eat when they take physical form, and they only take physical form when they walk the Earth."

"And you think they might actually leave mankind alone one day?"

Christian shrugged. "I don't know, but until these Evangelists quit stirring up trouble we shall never know."

The air was suddenly heavy and cold and the Tracers could see the mist of their breath in front of them. The hint of sulfur and decay grew to a full-on stench as if the carcass of an animal were rotting before their very noses. A carnal growl rolled from the tree-line across the road, and Christian could see the fear in Faithful's eyes.

"Come. Stay behind me and let me do the talking." Faithful nodded his pale face once and fell into step, keeping his eyes on the ground. As they crossed the road, a set of orange eyes glared out from behind a tree, followed by two more sets just behind. An eerie glow was just strong enough for Christian to make out the lines of their heads, each a different shape.

"Your servants are here, my lord Belial," greeted Christian.

The demon that Christian had addressed stepped out further from the tree line, if "step" was the right word. Although it was mostly covered by shadows at present (like the rest of its body), in the moonlight the Tracers could make out ornately decorated etched designs in the demon's animal-skull-like head—if it was a head and not some sort of intricate mask—casting an even more powerful effect than the engraving on Christian's breastplate, which now appeared to glow a dull red. Belial's etchings were met with a pair of grotesque steer-like horns protruding from the forehead of the skull. Thick black smoke enveloped the demons at nearly all times, especially from torso to legs, giving the impression that they floated like phantoms above the ground. And because these demonkind usually roamed about the Earth in the shadows of night, Christian had only caught rare glimpses of their blackened bodies in full daylight. They had gangly but powerful necks and appendages with ink-black skin that looked scarred—or charred by fire—and they wore layers of ragged blood-red linens that were wound around them tightly, like a wrapped corpse, underneath billowing black robes. Most memorable, though, were their eyes. Demonkind wore human eyes when they walked the human world. Without them, they would be pulled back down into the fiery depths of Mount Apollyon; into their realm. This was their great weakness—a secret that Christian had discovered in his youth.

Though they were difficult to make out in this light, Christian could see that each demon resembled the appearance of a different animal. Belial had goat-like features (or maybe they were more bull-like...?) including dark, curly fur and cloven hooves. One of his demon underlings had distinctly bird-like features, including inky feathers, while the other looked powerful and furry, like a bear. The reason for their animal-like and often-changing appearances was a secret that Christian had not yet uncovered. Demons were identifiable by the unique crests they wore upon their darkened steel breastplates and, if one were familiar enough with the creatures, by their unique voices.

DEMON
MASTERS

"There is a small party in a clearing beneath the cliff," Christian informed his superiors. "There are only four but they are all Evangelists—newly recruited by the way they have ordered their camp and huddle together so closely. But this carelessness could well be a trap so I would suggest you come at them against the wind from the southeast and fall upon them before they know what has struck."

The demons immediately set off into the night more quickly than they had arrived. Christian doubted that his assistant would understand now, but he hoped that Faithful would one day take some measure of solace in the swiftness of the Evangelists' deaths.

* * *

Christian and Faithful were "rewarded" for their thorough work with orders to serve Belial for another three months, which brought them quickly to the woods north of Temporal City where they remained on patrol. The heat had been less of a problem than the thick air that never seemed to dissipate with the hot sun— except for when the demon-commanders were around, which was really no comfort. The Tracers' days were a monotonous repetition: tracking Evangelists (and any other fugitive human prey), burying or cremating the devoured corpses after each feeding, hunting and foraging the woods for their own food, and, for Christian, restless sleep filled with nightmares of his family's demise in the violent eruption of Mount Apollyon.

Faithful increasingly refused to be of help in the actual Tracing, at least when the demons were not present. He was not incapable nor a coward, which he had proved as a soldier before becoming a Tracer, he was simply unwilling to be an accomplice to what he considered murder. At the same time, he was more and more often first at the site after a demon feeding to dispose of the bodies of the slain. For his part, Christian did whatever he could to make sure that the demons never found out about Faithful's moral objections.

After these three months, Belial still gave the Tracers no indication that they were to be relieved by another party.

27

Christian sighed as he watched Faithful rekindle their campfire that would now be used by the demons for another purpose: entrance into this world after their daily retreat to their own. Faithful looked at Christian for the briefest moment and Christian used the opportunity to give the order that he knew Faithful was not eager to hear.

"The fire will hold and it is almost sunset," he said. "We better get started."

Faithful inhaled a deep breath and exhaled it slowly. Weeks ago that sigh precluded the question of, "How much longer?" He clearly had tired of Christian's honest but unhelpful response that he did not know.

Wielding their swords, the Tracers set out to the northwest. After nearly three hours, a set of tracks in the ground finally looked promising. It was late into the night and as Christian knelt down to study the impressions in the dirt, he could sense by the tang of brimstone in the breeze that their demon overseers were following from a distance.

"Christian," Faithful whispered, "why the need to feed so often as of late?"

Christian shook his head. "I'm not sure. I have never known them to need such frequent meals. Perhaps they're more active than usual."

"What do they do in their world when they're not feeding?"

"I don't know," Christian needed no time to contemplate an answer. He often wondered what business demons undertook between feedings. "Sleep perhaps," he continued, though he seriously doubted that the creatures spent much time sleeping.

The most alarming trend, in light of their increasing appetites: the demons were frequently maiming and feeding on *any* flesh that happened to be wandering the forest trail unprepared, even animal flesh. Unfortunately, animal meat didn't seem to satiate the demons' hunger but merely provided temporary amusement while they awaited human flesh. Christian was convinced that this was an attempt at preventing the Tracers from having enough food to placate their own hunger, which was another constant reminder of the purpose they served to demonkind.

Christian could see his breath. The demon taskmasters were closer and, judging by the number of footprints in sight, it was shaping up to be a good night for them. Belial approached from the moonlight shadows, towering above Christian with his pitch black arms dangling inhumanly in a posture of taut readiness, with his two comrades not far behind. Christian briefly wondered, not for the first time, if their appearances might have something to do with past meals of impatience.

"We grow hungrier by the minute! I suggest you find our next meal, or you will become it!" Belial's voice was deep and inhuman and at the same time sounded both dangerously close and quite distant. The words hissed through razor-sharp teeth.

"If you eat me," Christian replied without looking up from the tracks, "who will find your meal tomorrow?"

Belial growled ferociously and Faithful recoiled, but Christian had learned by now to be much less intimidated when they addressed him with abstract threats. Even so, he wouldn't normally have been so brazen, but he suspected that his well-honed skills were too important to Belial to be merely digested by an impatient appetite. He had felt the need to confirm his suspicions that their prolonged service meant an increased demand in his Tracing services, and he was now satisfied. He would make no further attempt at testing the limits of his value to demonkind.

Christian indicated the footprint trail while Faithful went further up the road.

"They must be close." Christian pointed a finger to specific sets of prints. "There are a good number of Evangelists in this party and they've probably camped in the woods for the night."

"I think they went over that way," Faithful called back, motioning with a finger off the trail to one side where the edge of the tree line met the path.

Christian nodded and gave no indication about how baffled he was that Faithful suddenly seemed to be taking an active role in the future demise of more of Yeshua's radicals. Standing up straight, Christian said to the demon-commander, "Wait here and we'll scout it out." Christian turned from the beast so he did not have the image in his mind to accompany the deadly and impatient growl that emanated from Belial's vile mouth. He found Faithful waiting for him. Faithful seemed eager and Christian wondered if the younger Tracer may have snapped under the pressure of his assignment.

29

Christian placed a hand on Faithful's shoulder just as he was about to start into the wood. "Are you okay, my friend? Why so eager tonight?"

Faithful looked at him but said nothing. Christian could see a brimming excitement in his assistant's eyes.

"Do not do anything foolish," Christian warned. "Whatever is happening out in the wider world, we still have security among these ranks. In fact, at the moment we seem invaluable."

Christian held Faithful's gaze for several moments to see what affect his words would have, or to perhaps try to discern any hint of madness. The fire in Faithful's eyes did not dim, but Christian could do nothing about it except hope that the Tracer would keep his head.

"You follow my lead," Christian said finally. There was a pause and Faithful clenched his jaw, nodding in agreement. Christian held his position for one more moment, putting as much warning in his eyes as he could muster. Then they were off into wooded darkness so thick that even the moon could hardly penetrate in all its power.

The Tracers stalked their way from trunk to trunk toward the glow of what must be a campfire. Less than a hundred paces away, there was a *snap* of a dead branch underfoot. Christian froze and threw an angry look back at Faithful, but his companion shook his head, emphatically denying the silent charge that the careless noise had been his mistake. Christian believed him. He made hand signals communicating that Faithful was to pause where he was. Then from his own position Christian looked around as best he could in what little the shrouded moonlight revealed. The only consolation was that whoever the sentry was for the enemy, he or she could see no better than Christian. The key advantage Christian possessed as a seasoned Tracer was that he was exceedingly patient.

Christian's patience was rewarded after only a minute or two. A scout for the rebel group emerged from behind some low-growing foliage, likely content that his misstep had not given him away. Christian looked at Faithful and drew a line across his neck while shaking his head: the sign that the scout was *not* to be engaged. Their only task was information gathering and Christian hated killing any man when it served so little purpose.

30

Once the scout had passed them and disappeared into the darkness, Christian and Faithful moved forward slowly and with confidence in every step until they nearly reached the edge of the trees in this part of the wood. Christian stopped just at the perimeter of the shadows being cast by the handful of fires that burned warmly within the camp, which was situated on the outskirts of a vast meadow.

It was a moderate gathering of Evangelists. Some of the women among them were dressed in grey tunics, but most were dressed in the customary brown robes. All totaled there were about a dozen rebels—one of the larger travelling groups Christian had seen in a long while. He wondered how long they had been on the road and where they had come from.

Christian surveyed the scene: bedrolls were laid out close together, a larger cooking fire, which was more responsible for lighting the camp than the much smaller fires, was being tended and would surely be put out before long, and no other scouts were apparent but Christian expected there might be at least one more covering the far side of the site. Christian focused on the environment outside the encampment and shook his head. To the north the forest curved around and became one with the dark night, and about a half mile away to the south arose a tall face of craggy rocks. Cliffs to block them in and a dense forest inhabited by demons and wild beasts before them. Why were these followers of Yeshua so stubborn and arrogant? Were they foolish?

Christian looked back at Faithful and motioned that they were to return to Belial immediately with their report. The return trip always seemed to take less time than arriving at their destination, but this was unlikely the sentiment of Belial and his two companions—what were their names?—who seemed lethargic with ravenous hunger by the time he and Faithful returned. Seeing them sway like starved animals made Christian feel very fortunate that they were arriving with news that the fiends would find to their liking.

"A campsite of about twelve men and women, with at least one scout. Approach them from the meadow and the wood. Their campsite backs into rocky cliffs." Christian thought a moment, and then added: "They'll have nowhere to run if you hit them quickly."

Their demon taskmasters were off at once, with only three wisps of dissipating smoke to mark where they had been only a moment before. Christian placed a hand on the back of his neck. He looked after the trail on the road that he and Faithful had followed into the forest and as usual decided to wait a while before following. There was no need to be present for what would surely be a horrific feeding. By Christian's design, Faithful had never witnessed a feeding from up close and more often than not the men only witnessed the gruesome aftermath.

After some time had passed, maybe even an hour, Christian slapped the back of his hand against Faithful's chest.

"Come on," he said warily, and the Tracers moved at a slow pace along the path they had previously taken into the woods. When they had nearly arrived at the place where they had met the scout, a bright flare of firelight from the site of the camp brightened the whole area for several seconds and Christian could have sworn that the emblem on his breastplate blazed as well before shaking off of the strange thought. This was followed by screams and groans that turned the blood in Christian's body to frost. He looked over his shoulder and found that Faithful was standing stiff as a board with widened eyes.

Christian did not know how long either of them had stood as statues on their spots, Faithful's knees locked in horror and disgust, but it seemed as though an hour had passed before there were no longer any human cries emanating from the Evangelist camp. Christian took a careful step forward, and then another (he presumed Faithful was following his lead) until the encampment lay before them. Immediately, Christian regretted bringing Faithful to the horrific scene.

Immediately Christian noticed that there were not three demons feeding, but four! The demons were too busy feasting on their prey like wild animals to notice the arrival of the Tracers, but Christian still fought the desire to draw his sword in self-defense. Fortunately, Apollyon's demonkind never seemed to care much about presence of Tracers—they were only interested in filling their ravenous appetites for human flesh. Besides, upon seeing the chaos of such camps and the massacre of bodies, who would want to contend with such depraved beings?

Faithful's shoulder brushed against Christian's, causing Christian to glance at his assistant, who was looking off to the right. Christian followed Faithful's gaze to see the body of an Evangelist, still moving about weakly in the largest fire, which he must have been thrown into—*alive*—by a demon. The images of the town of Mansoul beneath the hellish smoke of Mount Apollyon, and the diabolical things that he witnessed taking place there less than a year before, leapt to the forefront of Christian's mind. This, joined with the horrific scene and the wet sounds of the demons moving their grotesque visages into the flesh of the dead was nearly more than he could stomach, however there was only so much sympathy that Christian would allow himself to feel for the Evangelists, no matter how awfully they died. After all, he had given up his own rebellion when the cost had grown too high. These Evangelists were fools and it was their fault that Christian was separated from his family.

With another flare from the fire containing the Evangelist's body, a demonic breastplate rolled out of the fire and what could only be described as smoky appendages began to drag the armor toward the nearest demon. Christian watched in horror as the armor then grew a shadowy, skull-like head. The nearby demon reached out its claw and placed a set of *human eyes* into the shadowy eye sockets and the smoky figure took on flesh and appeared as any other demon. The fifth demon immediately began feeding.

Then Christian saw another horrifying sight: Belial was placing what looked like a pair of human eyes into a small, engraved box that he then placed inside a hidden pocket in his robe. One of the new demons did the same. In fact, Christian now noticed that *none* of the Evangelists still possessed their eyes.

Next to Christian, Faithful doubled over and retched violently at the dismal, brutish scene that was playing out before them, and likely also at the disgust and guilt of more than three months of being party to this heinous work. This was certainly the worst scene to confront Faithful so far.

Christian patted his fellow Tracer on the back and brought him into the high grass of the meadow to allow him the opportunity to calm his mind. He privately wondered if Faithful would ever recover from this.

Christian faced east and noted the cobalt hue of that horizon. Another day was nearly upon them and Faithful would need every one of the approaching hours to find a way to carry on in the service of Apollyon.

The Tracer looked again at his vile taskmasters, then back at the horizon. Their blood-lust would distract them from seeing the sunrise, and demons *hated* direct sunlight. It seemed to affect each demon to varying degrees, but Christian had often seen demons flee in panic from the sun's presence. He sucked in a deep, tired breath and let it out slowly, trying to think of his family. This was all for their safety; there was nothing in Christian's world but those he loved so deeply. He believed there was nothing he would not do to protect them.

"My lords," Christian announced to no response. He spoke louder, "Lord Belial! Daylight approaches." As if on cue, the demons growled in frustration and stood from their meals. Belial approached Christian so aggressively that Christian instinctively reached for his sword, a gesture which fortunately seemed to go unnoticed by the demon that was checking to make sure that the contents of its bloodied pocket were secure.

"Be ready at first dark," Belial growled in his monstrous voice, "and keep this fire burning." Belial was joined by his companions and then all five approached the largest remaining campfire, inside of which the discarded corpse of the Evangelist was charring. Belial growled with ferocity and the flames leapt into the air. In an instant, the demons dove one-by-one into their world through the newly-consecrated fire portal.

Faithful wiped his mouth and looked up into Christian's stunned gaze. "Five," Faithful said, "there were five of them."

CHAPTER FOUR

"Christian, how do you do this?"

Christian was facing away from Faithful and had nearly managed to find sleep beneath the shade of trees nearby the Evangelists' encampment, which would shield him from the sun as it tracked across the sky. He knew what Faithful was inquiring about and was not pleased at the thoughts that were now bound to again flood his mind.

"I lie down, close my eyes—"

"You know what I mean! How do you hunt for *them*? After all these years..." Faithful interrupted. Christian opened his eyes but kept his back turned.

"My family," he replied. "I do this for Christy and Matthew and Sammie and Joseph." He heard Faithful rustling on his bedroll and presumed that he had lain back down. Christian closed his eyes when he was confident that the prolonged silence meant the young man had accepted his answer.

"What makes us better than them—the people we hunt for Apollyon?" Faithful asked in a soft voice.

"Better? We're just more fortunate. We have a choice. They don't."

"So they're livestock to be rounded up for the slaughter? And we're...what...?"

Christian exhaled loudly in exasperation.

"We are *not* livestock."

Christian knew it was too much to expect that Faithful had finished. Christian sympathized with the weight of the previous night's horrors on his young companion's mind, but he was exhausted.

"They sure keep us close if we're not livestock," said Faithful.

Christian considered the troubling notion and then did his best to shake it from his mind. The young man had a point, though his understanding of Apollyon's reign was overly simplistic.

"What kind of 'good master' threatens a family, or a life, to ensure loyalty?" Faithful continued.

"Who says a master must be good? I have read some from the Law of El Shaddai—"

"What law?" Faithful interrupted.

"The Evangelists often carry Books that they claim were written by their God, Himself—through men—instructing them in how mankind should live. It is a death sentence to have any such Book in your possession. How do you not know this?" Christian did not wait long for a response. "When I was younger and much more foolhardy, I found one of these Books and read a bit from it about the threats to generations for any that break even one measure of El Shaddai's commands. Do you find this more comforting than what Apollyon requires?"

Faithful was silent for a moment. "His followers seem to, given what they face from Apollyon for opposing him." Faithful paused, and Christian waited for him to continue. "I realize that we risk our lives as well, but we serve demonkind out of fear of losing our lives...our homes and families. What reason do the followers of Yeshua have for facing the horrors we have witnessed? They are always outnumbered, and yet they continue on. Wouldn't they rather live in peace, as we would?"

Christian half-turned so that Faithful could see at least one of his eyes. "I wish they would. Maybe they fear the wrath of El Shaddai even more than we realize. Does it really matter *why* they tempt fate?" Christian knew it always mattered *why,* but he was trying to end the conversation quickly. "They are *rebels,* Faithful. Traitors against the laws of men under the rule of Apollyon and as a result they make all of our lives more difficult. Not even Evangelists can keep the Law that El Shaddai has made for them, so they stand as much condemned to the abyss as we do by their reasoning. Perhaps future generations may look at our lives with admiration if we are seen to have lived in service and loyalty to our families and neighbors. After all, a rebel does not only risk his own life..."

36

Christian trailed off as he couldn't help but think about how costly his own rebellion had been. He finally continued after a moment of silent reflection. Nothing I know about the life of a follower of Yeshua is worth the kind of suffering and death His followers must endure in this world, nor is it worth causing pain to so many others. Indeed, if we are all doomed to suffer after this life, I would at least live in this world with as much comfort as possible."

"But why would these 'rebels' suffer such terrible pains in this world, and defy Apollyon, if their end was hopeless? There must be more—"

"You may suffer in eternity, if indeed there is an afterlife—though I see no evidence of it—or be one of *them* and surely suffer both here *and* evermore!" Christian continued, "There is nothing further on this subject, except this: you are on evening fire duty."

Christian watched Faithful swallow his words like a lump of dry bread. Then he lay down and turned away from Faithful. Satisfied that he was now done arguing, Christian returned his thoughts to sleep, but now its prospects seemed further than ever as memories from his past swirled around in Christian's mind and drudged up long-repressed feelings of dissatisfaction toward the world as it now was and a longing for a better world that seemed as though it could never be.

Another thought was also puzzling Christian: the demons were recruiting. They were increasing their Earth-walking ranks and Christian could not help but wonder why. It was normal for demons to keep a standing presence in the world of men to keep the Evangelist ranks at bay, but why the need for *more*? He had only seen this behavior once before: during his rebellion when Christian and his comrades had so successfully diminished the demon ranks that they were forced to travel greater distances to regroup and expend more energy during battle.

Christian hadn't heard any recent news of great success by the rebels against Apollyon, so why were the demons acting as though they were either preparing for, or in the midst of, a great battle?

Another option came to mind, and that was that the demons might be increasing their ranks in order to escalate the conflict.

This was a possibility of some intrigue. Where were Belial and his demon companions going when they weren't feeding? Were they returning to their fiery shadow realm to plot evil? Were they travelling to another earthly location further than they could travel by land? Christian had more questions than he thought could ever be answered, but he felt as certain as he could about one thing: the demon armies are advancing—they must be.

All these thoughts of a prolonged war were wearying to Christian. Given the amount of bodies he had buried, Christian felt certain that the rebels stood almost no chance against their attackers—or so it seemed. Perhaps the Evangelists were nearing defeat and Apollyon was attempting to deal a forceful deciding blow. Perhaps he was preparing for a final attack on Yeshua's lands.

This all made the words of his friend Faithful ring even more true to Christian: if these seditionists *willingly* faced certain death or capture when attacked by Apollyon's servants, what could be so valuable to be worth enduring this promise of defeat? Christian knew of El Shaddai, and His decrees were no less burdensome or exacting (even if they were moral) than those of Apollyon—for they not only judged a man in this world but also set him up for doom in the next if even one command was broken. Why not simply accept the rule of Apollyon if his victory was so certain? There must have been much about this war that Christian didn't know.

So what was it about El Shaddai's Son, Yeshua, that allegedly made tribulations and death out to be mere obstacles? Such a hope seemed folly unless Yeshua made the keeping of His Father's Law somehow achievable. Christian was sure that *none* could keep the Law of El Shaddai, how could anyone live up to such a "Righteous Code"? Therefore El Shaddai must be forced to condemn countless numbers of His own Son's followers. Perhaps El Shaddai merely allowed Evangelists to be destroyed at Apollyon's hand as a form of judgment.

With these perplexing questions and paradoxes pummeling his mind, sleep ambushed Christian, promising him a slumber that would be far from restful...

The nightmare-vision that had cursed Christian and burdened his soul since his last trip to Mansoul faded into view, as if someone had lit a lamp in a room and quickly fed it more oil...

Christy smiled at Christian, then swiftly directed her gaze to Sammie who was being chased by Matthew. Somehow she captured the children in one arm while holding Joseph, and laughed with them, pulling both children into a line to greet their father in front of the family home.

Christian was on all fours crawling toward his family in pain that could not be discovered, and only defined as a crushing weight upon his back. His arms and shoulders and chest ached, his breathing stung when he could catch a full breath at all. He feared that each placement of a hand or knee would result in those bones shattering, and it was for this fear that he continued on toward his family as quickly as possible. He must warn them! But his family could not see his anguish, or their own danger. Their ignorant joy mocked his suffering and he wanted to weep. Behind their cottage Mount Apollyon rumbled, not pleased with being ignored by Christian and his family. Christian's eyes flicked to it immediately and then back to his family: they gave no indication that they had heard even a rustling of the air.

Suddenly, Mount Apollyon erupted—chunks of earth, molten rock, smoke, and ash were propelled into the sky in all directions and then arched back toward the surrounding terrain. The debris picked up speed as it approached Destruction, although everything else around Christian now seemed to move at a snail's pace. The fiery missiles of creation nearest the earth began crashing into the city, followed by those that had been thrown the highest and farthest into the air. The closer these elements came the better Christian could make out what he thought was merely smoke behaving in an unnatural manner: dark spirits were falling with the pieces of Mount Apollyon, adding to the horror of the scene as they entered the city. Human screams joined their carnal snarls. One by one Christian watched as the homes of neighbors were obliterated by the firestorm Armageddon and demonic evil. Christian and his home were in the clear path of this deadly reckoning!

Christian's eyes widened as he tried to call out to Christy to flee, but his cry was silent and went unheard by his wife and children. They looked at him, yet remained blind and deaf to his warning. He tried again, but his desperation only seemed to increase their serene joy, and the next moment they and the fire and the demons joined and were no more—

Christian awoke on his back with a shudder, sweating, out of breath, and unable to shake the fear of eminent danger. He picked up his head to study the shadows and concluded that he had not been asleep much more than an hour. He looked to the side and was relieved to see that Faithful, his back turned, had apparently not had his sleep disturbed. Christian rolled onto his side so that he faced away from Faithful, breathed in the wonderful scent of woodland air, and again succumbed to his exhaustion.

CHAPTER FIVE

"—up Christian!"

The veteran Tracer's hand was upon the grip of his sword before his eyes were even open, and he was nearly as quickly on his feet.

"Over here—you have got to see this!" Faithful said with panic in his voice.

The years of tracking in the wilderness had made it second nature to quickly shake away his grogginess, and Christian saw with clear eyes that Faithful was standing in the shadow of the wood ahead. Christian looked back over his shoulder, past the fire burning in the center of the now desolate rebel campsite, then up to study the sky. Dusk was fast approaching—only a sliver of the setting sun remained on the horizon.

"You have to see this!" Faithful called again.

Leaving his helmet behind in his haste, Christian arrived beside his companion and knelt down to see the area that Faithful indicated with a finger. Christian stood back to his feet after only a moment of study and flicked his eyes toward the road from where they had come the previous evening.

"Someone got away," Christian said. "Stay here."

Christian went back to their camp for a pair of torches. He lit the torches in the decent campfire that was burning nearby and hastily returned to Faithful with them.

Faithful wasted no time and set out on the trail of blood that was nearly a day old with Christian close behind. The trail had started directly for the road, but it gently turned so that the wounded person was moving parallel to the main travelling path.

Night was quickly approaching. If they were fortunate they would have maybe ten minutes to determine if there truly had been a survivor before Belial and his cohort arrived for another night of hunting. And how many demons would they need to find meals for tonight?

Suddenly it seemed very unlikely to Christian that he and Faithful would be relieved of their duties anytime soon. Even if they were, how much time would they have with their families before their next patrol? Christian was accustomed to full seasons of reprieve from being a Tracer which he relied on to harvest his crops and feed his family. How could they live with anything less? Resentment toward the Evangelists continued to grow as Christian longed for home.

"There!" Faithful turned his head partly toward Christian and then jerked it forward. Christian had also seen the form against the tree just before his companion had pointed it out, and was already shifting his sword so that it could be quickly wielded.

The wounded man appeared to be from the same party of Evangelists that the Tracers had set Belial upon the night prior. Blood from a terrible wound, which by now had largely dried due to dwindling supply, stained the man's hand and his dirt-brown robe. The rebel was dying; his body had no more blood to pour.

But this was not the most remarkable sight to meet Christian's eyes. Despite the graveness of his situation, the face of the Evangelist wore nothing but a veil of peace. His eyes were open and Christian knew he could see the Tracers—could see their armor which bore emblems of Apollyon, his great enemy. And yet there was no hint of terror or spiteful wrath. The Evangelist simply seemed to know that his time on this Earth was at its end, and his peacefulness shattered any notion Christian held that Evangelists were forced into service by El Shaddai as he and Faithful were by Apollyon. Were Christian to face his end on the battlefield, any solace he would find in giving his life for the protection of his family would be negated by his fear for their safety in his absence.

Christian could have no peace.

In spite of his resentment, Christian pulled forth his sword and moved to a position that would execute a clean strike across the Evangelist's neck but not decapitate: a mercy killing.

"NO!" Faithful's opposing cry echoed off the trees and shattered the otherwise eerily serene atmosphere.

EVANGELIST

FLEE FROM THE WRATH TO COME

Christian did not lower his sword, nor did he take his eyes from the Evangelist.

"Stand down, you *fool!* It will be far better for this rebel if his life is ended quickly, before our lords arrive."

"No!" Faithful repeated as insistently as the first time and placed himself between Christian and the dying man with arms spread wide. "I have questions!"

The Tracers faced off for a moment and Faithful's eyes held genuine fear and desperation. He is afraid that I will kill him, Christian thought, hurt that his protégé feared the possibility of death at his hand. He lowered his blade.

As Faithful turned and fell to both knees before the rebel, Christian tried to determine why his friend was actually prepared to die for the opportunity to speak with one who was identified as their enemy. Is this my fault? He wondered. Have I planted ideas in his head or left too many questions unanswered? Since the death of Faithful's father, Christian had always felt the need to protect Faithful and Deedee—in fact, he'd promised to do so. Faithful's father died before he had the opportunity to share his conversion to belief in Yeshua with his family, and Christian believed that if he kept his old friend's conversion a secret, the danger would die with him. But now, Faithful seemed as desperate for answers as his father had been so many years before. How could this be?

"Are you...are you an Evangelist?" Faithful asked in a tone that most would have interpreted as reverent.

The Evangelist nodded, but he did not wince at the pain he surely must have felt. Instead, he stared deeply—compassionately—into Faithful's eyes.

Faithful passed his torch to the other hand, then inserted his free hand beneath the back of his armor plate and pulled out a dirty and beaten object. The Evangelist's eyes widened and his lips turned into the faintest smile at the site of a Book. Christian on the other hand, was mortified. He had barely recovered from the first shock that came from Faithful's brave challenge to his authority and his own failure to protect the young man from this treason, but seeing a copy of a Book of El Shaddai in the hands of one sworn to serve Apollyon sent cold chills up and down his spine. This was a death sentence! Every muscle in Christian's body screamed to rip the Book from Faithful's hands, but none would actually move to carry out the action. He was immediately angry with himself for telling

Faithful that he had once read from the Law. As far as he was concerned, if Faithful was caught with the Book and punished, it would be Christian's fault and so much of what he had fought for years to protect would be lost.

"This Book says that we need not fear death because your King has conquered it," Faithful began. "Is this true?"

The Evangelist nodded and proceeded to speak despite the obvious difficulty.

"Yes... His Kingdom is eternal... Yeshua loves His people... He will save them all. The gate to His...Kingdom…is opened for *any* who will hearken to His call and follow Him." The man took several heavy breaths and motioned his head slightly toward the emblem on Faithful's chest. "Apollyon's days are numbered. The King is returning to reclaim this land and His people forever...never again to be terrorized by Apollyon and his unrepentant servants."

"This is *treason*! Your kind passes over many borders spreading these lies, trying to stoke the dying flame of what was once a raging rebellion and destroying so many lives in the process," Christian managed in as hushed a voice as possible under the circumstances. He needed to end this conversation quickly, but he knew it would only truly end if he found a way to satisfy Faithful's curiosity. "Can you not leave us in peace? Yeshua has been said to be coming for countless years. That you whisper sedition and hopeless folly from lips soon to be lifeless is little more than wanton desire to drag us and our families into darkness with you!"

The Evangelist turned, a spark kindled in his eyes. "As you say, servant of Apollyon, these lips will soon speak no more. To what end would lies serve me now? If I desired your destruction I would be silent and not waste my final breaths in this world trying to warn you! I am *not* the rebel in this war."

While Christian attempted to process the Evangelist's claim, he felt a familiar chill sweep across his neck and the faintest tinge of sulfur warned him that the moment he feared had arrived. He was out of time and must protect Faithful.

Immediately, Christian tore the Book from Faithful's grip and shoved his surprised companion to the ground just as a vicious snarl erupted from behind the Tracers and a spear meant for Faithful pinned the Evangelist to a tree. Dark blood oozed from the man's mouth and the new wound smoldered from the heat of the demonic blade, and yet the Evangelist's pleading eyes still held Christian's gaze with a miraculous clarity.

"Your...true enemy...is all around you.... Flee...! Flee from the wrath...to come!"

The Evangelist's eyes stared off to a point beyond this present realm and became lifeless. It was a sight that Christian could never get used to, no matter how many times he had the misfortune of witnessing death.

"*Hu*-man! What is that in your hand?"

Belial's voice was deadly and yanked Christian's attention back to his immediate danger, and he looked at the Book in his hand to which the demon was referring. The Tracer knew that Belial's question was more of an accusation. There was no use trying to explain. Demons rarely had much use for the truth and they never forgave.

Christian raised his head and squared his jaw with some defiance while his body carried mostly stiff resignation. It had been a long time since he had reflected upon how his service to Apollyon might come to a final end. He no longer needed to speculate.

With one taloned hand, Belial grabbed Christian by the chains that crossed his armor and with unnatural power lifted him off the ground by nearly a foot. The demon thrust his other taloned hand around the Tracer's throat and began to slowly constrict. Christian grabbed the arm of the hand wrapped around his neck with both of his own, causing him to drop both his sword and the Book. Belial glanced at the fallen objects. It took only a moment for him to confirm which Book had fallen from Christian's possession.

A low and fully intimidating growl rolled out of the demon-lord's muzzle as he slowly turned back to his captive. His flaming eyes squinted as he likely considered whether a Tracer of so many campaigns could really be so brainless, or if perhaps the veteran tracker had always been a rebel out to make him look like a fool before Apollyon and the rest of his demonkind.

Whatever he decided, Christian was sure he was no longer invaluable to Belial and it would not be a quick end for him or Faithful. Belial clenched his jaw, noted that his dark brothers—only two of them—now flanked him, and then tightened his grip on Christian's throat with one intent: leave just enough life in him for Christian to feel himself being devoured alive. Christian wondered if his eyes would be removed. If so, would he be alive when it happened? Already the Tracer could feel the sharp talons puncture his neck as hazy blackness crowded at the edges of his vision while less and less air was permitted into his lungs.

A terrible scream erupted from Belial and Christian found himself carelessly dropped to his hands and knees with Belial squirming before him. Air rushed down Christian's throat only to be evicted by violent and uncontrollable spasms of hacking and his rage was finally fully rekindled as, in an instant, he thought of his hatred for demonkind, his resentment toward the Evangelists for forcing him to fight a war not his own, and his frustration with how little control he had over his own life.

With shrieks of rage, the two standing demons were upon Faithful, who had come to Christian's defense by stabbing Belial through the image of Apollyon emblazoned on its breastplate. Christian's hand found his sword in an instant and just as quickly his blade was thrust into Belial's eyes, which caused minor eruptions of flame to burst forth from the demon's eye sockets before the demon dissolved into lifeless smoke. Only its breastplate, bearing the emblem of Apollyon, remained. Next, Christian rolled, narrowly avoiding the downward attack of a demon's blade. Immediately his concern was for his friend. The clanging of swords confirmed that Faithful was defending himself admirably, sword against talons, but it would not be enough: the young Tracer had never been matched against one of Apollyon's demonkind. Christian on the other hand, had.

Christian focused on his own opponent, who allowed hate to consume him, resulting in random thrusts and wild slashes from his demon blade. Christian waited for one of the demon's wild thrusts, then used the curve on the upper part of his own blade to hook and pin the demon's weapon to the dirt in one swift motion. Next came a vicious, indefensible slash across the eyes which again sent another small shower of flames, followed by dark smoky residue, from the monster's face in all directions. This demon also disappeared into lifeless smoke, leaving behind another breastplate.

The Tracer turned from his dispatched adversary to lend aid to Faithful. The younger man was on his back, his sword hopelessly jammed across his stomach as the demon pressed down one-handed with his own and attempted to claw at Faithful's face with the other.

"You will not take my eyes!" Faithful shouted in frenzied fear.

Either Faithful's diabolical foe was too preoccupied with Faithful or he was too arrogant to take note of the situation of his fellow demons but, whatever the case, Christian thrust his sword into the demon's eye sockets with a shout of rage. The demon bent back in a wail of anguish as Christian removed his blade and then Christian watched as it rolled around in its own black fog like a fish out of water until if finally left behind a third breastplate, returning to the world of demons in the depths of Mount Apollyon.

While catching his breath, Christian took stock of the three beaten fiends who had been their masters. They were now still but for the heavy smoke that scattered with the wind.

"Their eyes are their weakness," Christian mustered through heavy breathing.

Faithful joined his mentor with three deep scratches across the back of his neck that revealed his new experience as a demon slayer. He wore an amazed look, but once the rush from the duel wore off Christian knew it would quickly fade to dread.

"What have we done?" Christian said, soberness already reflecting in his own voice.

"How long until they are given new bodies?" Faithful asked, knowing well that while the physical bodies demons inhabited could be destroyed (though before now not knowing how), demon souls could not be killed by human weapons.

49

Christian's response was even and came with a slight shrug and the flash of a scowl. "No telling yet. It depends on how valuable they are to Apollyon." Christian thought it best not to mention that the demon-lord was certainly not limited to sending only Belial after them. Then a new realization came roaring to his mind.

"My family..."

Faithful's eyes widened: "I'm sorry, Christian. I thought we were... I had—"

"Hush, man! Let me think!" Christian considered their options and looked at the sky through the tree canopy finding parts of two specific constellations: the night was still young and they could not risk abandoning their provisions—and there was the matter of the fire portal. They had very little time, but if Belial and his fellow demons were not returned to this world too quickly, there was a chance that having no hint of human presence in the vicinity would throw off any who came to investigate. At the least, the demons would certainly have to travel a greater distance with no access to the fire portal. Therefore it was worth the risk of the few extra minutes it would take to gather their packs and extinguish the fire for any extra time it would buy them.

Beside him, Faithful was starting to look nervous, as Christian expected, and he knew that the uncontrollable trembling would now make Faithful impatient and slow-witted.

"We should go back to Destruction..." Faithful rambled, "…get your family and my mother...hide them—"

"Quiet!" Christian hoped that his harshness would startle the young man into silence. He was angry that he had allowed, and perhaps even encouraged, Faithful's foolish line of questioning. Christian tried not to focus on the painful irony that Faithful, the young man who he had spent years protecting and had sacrificed so much for, could be the cause of the death of Christian's own family.

"We cannot return home!" Christian growled. "We would never arrive before the demons. We would only *seal* their fates."

"If we don't save them, they will surely be tortured and killed!"

Christian turned to Faithful with the light of the two torches lying on the barren ground bearing their full effect on the Tracer as light and shadow played over the lines and creases of his face. Christian didn't need Faithful to tell him what happens to rebels' loved ones.

"Understand this: Apollyon makes traitors watch as his twisted servants..." The screams in his memories of Mansoul, and further back to the families of his former rebel comrades, wafted through Christian's mind, causing his pause to become a new course of explanation. "The further we are from our families, the longer they probably have on this Earth. We have been forced into a new course of action. We need to find *help* if there is to be any hope for them."

A distinct dark space in the middle of the firelight over Faithful's shoulder redirected Christian's attention: it was the Book. Christian moved to its position, returned his sword to its sheath on his back, and retrieved the tome. Faithful turned and carefully closed the two paces that separated him from his mentor. Christian allowed the fire to illuminate the Book's cover for just a few moments: there was nothing remarkable about the Book, nothing that indicated there was any great truth within its pages beyond that of any normal book Christian had ever seen, and yet he knew that to its adherents there was a vast difference. He thrust the battered collection of pages into the chest of his companion, and then looked at Faithful.

"I hope this Book was worth our lives."

CHAPTER SIX

BACK IN THE DUNGEON
AT DOUBTING CASTLE

John again held the Book up to where the dim torchlight shone strongest through the cracks in the cell door to examine it fully. It was a collection of bound pages similar in size to all the other Books John had ever seen. It was not very thick, but so many of them weren't in order to make them easier to hide away from opposing eyes. He picked the Book up and opened it, and the first words he saw brought confirmation. It was indeed a Book—John could finally say that he held one and, by an unknown grace, in a place that no forces of Apollyon would ever care to look.

He closed the Book and for a long moment did nothing but hold it in his hand, unsure of how to proceed. He was almost afraid of what he might find in its pages; that the words might not live up to the expectations that he had built in his mind over a lifetime. After all, people died for these words. Dare he hope...? Indeed, John was afraid to even *hope* in this dark and cruel place.

It took him several more minutes to find his courage but, finally, John again opened the book and began to read. The first Pages spoke cryptically:

In the beginning was the Word, and the Word was with God, and the Word was God. He was in the beginning with God.

All things came into being through Him, and apart from Him nothing came into being that has come into being.

In Him was life, and the life was the Light of men.

The Light shines in the darkness, and the darkness did not comprehend it.

The burning of deep emotion caught in John's throat and a cry releasing an ocean of pent-up long-suffering nearly escaped when his eyes fell upon the words: "*The Light shines in the darkness, and the darkness did not comprehend it.*"

He did not know anything further about this "Light", but the context could not have been more profound to John in his dark world, who otherwise only knew light from the dim torches on the other side of his prison door. Not even a pinhole of light could come into the cavernous dungeon from the outside world, and yet the words made John feel as though he was bathing in the radiance of ten suns, which he had not known for so long a time that it may as well have been an eternity.

John intended to read further, but a violent cough turned his attention to the man who now shared John's cell. John crawled back to the man, Book firmly in hand. He laid it down only to raise the soldier's head from the ground so that he might take a few sips of the brackish water that John had scooped up with a small tin bowl.

"Hello again," John greeted, with no response from his companion.

"So..." John continued in his desperate longing for conversation, "What brought you here, eh? Besides that Ogre, I mean."

The soldier's face twisted in disgust at the taste of the water, but John paid little attention.

"Look, what I mean is: where are you from?"

The man used what little moisture he had in his mouth to form one hoarse word: "Book."

John placed the man's head back on the ground and picked up the item indicated.

"Yes, I have your Book. You must have dropped it when our 'host' delivered you here. I hope you don't mind—being more than a bit lacking in my own reading material—I thought I'd have a read."

The soldier actually managed the faintest of smiles that passed so quickly John began to doubt it had even occurred. Another word came from the man: "Back..."

John flipped through the pages until the style of the printed text changed into that of handwriting. He found that many pages were filled with the writing, and at one point the script changed to a different hand that was easier to make out than the first.

"The first bit is somewhat difficult to make out," John replied as he looked up. "Perhaps it would be easier if you—"

Talking would be a waste of time for the present as John found that his new friend had fainted away from whatever had been his ordeal. But at least the soldier's breathing was slightly more smooth and easier to detect. He would need food, and soon, if there was to be any hope of a recovery. There was nothing more that could be done until then.

John located his favorite place against the wall, where a natural outcropping of rock both provided him with a hint of light through the door and also a refreshing breeze that swept up from the floor underneath the cell door at intermittent times. He opened the Book, which seemed to accentuate the light from the torch so that the pages glowed with a supernatural light. He flipped to where the handwriting became clearer and quickly settled in to read what he presumed was the journal of the man who had suddenly entered his world.

CHAPTER SEVEN

Run.

For the last seven hours this had been Christian and Faithful's best tactic. Avoiding the common roads out of necessity, there was no telling how many miles the Tracers' feet had carried them, at least not in the dark where there was nothing but forest above, trunks all around, and a carpet of pine needles and dirt that indicated it could go on forever. Better men than Christian had become hopelessly lost in such settings—and that was as far as the Tracer allowed himself to ruminate. As long as the eastern horizon stayed generally in their vision, they had a chance.

Run, from demon-masters that could find them if they lingered anywhere for too long.

Run, with packs chained to their backs and a single torch between the two of them.

Run.

In the pitch black and at the flurrying pace they needed to maintain, Christian tripped over a branch (it was nothing short of a miracle that it took so long for this to happen) and dropped the torch. Faithful had no time to avoid Christian's body as he impacted the ground. Faithful crashed on top of Christian, managing to also extinguish the torch with his body.

"Sorry," Faithful grunted, as if he was to blame, while he hurriedly surveyed his body for burns and swatted himself violently to make sure he would not catch aflame.

Neither man was injured by the fall, but they had lost their torch for the remainder of the night since lighting a new fire would be too risky given the amount of time it would take.

It seemed as good a time as any to take at least a short break, and so the men sat against a flat section of earth about waist high that was part of a sudden dip in the immediate terrain. Resting on the plateau above them, and providing additional cover, was the trunk of an old pine that looked to have fallen recently. Both men had stored their helmets in their packs—which they were painfully reminded of in the fall—because they needed unobstructed sight far more than protection.

At least here they could still try to get some prolonged and much-needed rest. Christian supposed many minutes had passed when—*SNAP!*

The Tracers dove flat against their dirt shelter. Faithful's eyes darted to Christian's for direction. Christian raised a finger to his lips for absolute stillness and silence. He held his finger there for several moments and then blew a deliberate breath out his mouth. Two visible mists, split by his finger, materialized. Faithful understood, even more so when the stench of sulfur and decay met their nostrils like no odor they had yet experienced.

Christian slowly raised his head to take a peek and Faithful followed his lead.

Not far from their position they spotted a tall, handsome man still a decade from middle age drifting among the trees. The coming of dawn's twilight made the pale skin on his face a ghostly ashen grey, which contrasted fiercely with his wavy dark hair. He wore armor—a distinct iron plate with raised markings that Christian could not discern from his line of sight. The unnatural black cloak that flowed (quite literally) behind him was made of no cloth found in this world: it was as thick smoke rolling upon the ground. The figure turned in their direction, causing Christian to duck quickly beneath the earthen cover.

Faithful lingered, unable to break his gaze from the sight, presumably in spite of the creeping chill along his spine and arms that Christian was feeling on his own person.

Christian dragged Faithful down beside him and both men waited, barely breathing, until the smell of pine and the clean air of the coming daybreak filled their senses. They waited another several minutes to be doubly cautious in light of their fugitive status, before rising from their place to see if the strange demon was indeed absent.

Their eyes confirmed that he had gone, and both men took in several deep breaths as they stood to stretch their limbs.

"Why were you lingering?" Christian asked.

Faithful shrugged. "I don't know, sir. I just...I've never seen a demon that looked so...human."

"It's a miracle you weren't seen. That was no ordinary demon, my friend. If there are *any* to wholly fear it is the 'flesh walkers' because they appear as we do—humankind."

"How can a demon look so human?"

"He was...wearing...a human body. Or at least a body that was once human," Christian explained in quite disgust.

Christian looked at Faithful and saw that his interest was very clear, and so he reluctantly continued. "I never spoke of them because I hoped we would not meet one. I've only done so myself, once." Christian unsuccessfully suppressed a shudder. "They are few, and they are powerful, certainly not to be contended with. I have heard it said that flesh walkers are 'the Fallen'—great Celestial warrior-princes who were once allies of El Shaddai from the Days Untold. He cursed these Celestial Beings, and the servants who supported them, for unforgivable betrayal." Christian paused to reflect on what the Evangelist had said about not being a rebel in this war. Indeed, the legends of the Fallen would indicate that Apollyon, himself, was the greatest rebel. That was, of course, if the legends could be believed. He continued, "The Fallen are all now forced to roam the world for sustenance to stay alive. I do not know their exact number, but I have learned a small number of the demon-lord names from those hushed conversations: Mammon and Leviathan, Diabolus (who conquered Mansoul) and their leader is—"

"Apollyon," Faithful finished.

Christian nodded his head, affirming the answer. "Did you see the crest upon this flesh walker's breastplate? It would have an appearance like the fanged head upon our own, but there would be a scorpion tail above the head, poised to strike, wings flanking the head and tail, all within a hollow sphere with nothing behind, like peering into an abyss. No other demon would have armor with all these as one emblem upon the breastplate." Even before Christian finished he knew his answer as the color drained from Faithful's face.

"Apollyon! It was King *Apollyon*! He is *here*! He has already come to investigate the attack upon his brothers. He will learn what we have done...!"

"Hush your *voice*! We cannot be sure why he is out here," Christian ordered through tensed teeth.

He needed to think. Why *would* Apollyon be out in these woods? Apollyon had never carried out an investigation personally so far as Christian had ever heard. During Christian's First Great Rebellion, Apollyon himself had never stepped foot onto a battlefield until his enemy was all but defeated and ready for judgment. That was the first and only time that Christian had ever met a flesh walker.

The Tracer could not fathom the demon-lord coming out into the wilderness in search of miscreants—he had underlings like Belial and the others for such work. So why would he be in these woods? Christian felt more helpless than ever to protect his family, and he was desperate to solve this puzzle that he believed could hold the only hope for their survival. He needed answers.

Christian looked around and was pleased to see that it was now light enough to distinguish trunks from their foliage. A pair of larks commenced a duet nearby, giving him rising courage because demonkind was rarely active in the sunlight. He hoped that flesh walkers would share this distaste for daylight.

"Follow me," he said to Faithful. "And be vigilant."

Christian led the way to the area where they had seen Apollyon, but a quick survey yielded nothing out of the ordinary. A draft of morning breeze swept past them, bringing with it the scent of burnt ash. Christian moved forward against the wind at a quick pace through a section of the wood that became dense with underbrush. They pushed aside low branches and continued to search for the source of this strange odor.

The men finally emerged into a small clearing and immediately halted at the sight of six maimed devoured human corpses, one likely an Evangelist by the familiar look of the shredded woolen robe, and many that were unidentifiable.

"What a monster," Faithful said under his breath. "That explains what he was doing here, I suppose. He was hungry." The tone of Faithful's voice indicated that he was clearly disgusted.

Christian did not face him. "Apollyon does not hunt his own food. At least he never did," said Christian, trailing off for a moment into silent thought before continuing. "His food is brought to him under the Mountain. None of this makes sense. Why would he be mucking around with reb—" Christian stopped, and his mind reeled. His human enemies had always been "rebels" (if not "traitors") before now. He again remembered Evangelist's words: "I am not the rebel in this war," he had said.

Suddenly the realization hit Christian with a wave of nausea, though it was not immediately noticeable due to the horrible state of the corpses.

"Look closer," Christian said.

"I don't think that's a good—" Faithful stopped short. "Their eyes. *Three* sets of eyes."

Indeed, Christian had noticed that of the six corpses devoured, only three seemed to have had their eyes removed: one for each demon slain that very night. The first glints of the sun caught Christian's eye as the beams cut through a light mist. "Come. We must keep moving."

Faithful did not move. He continued to gaze at the bodies. "What if we go back? Explain ourselves? What harm has been done, really? Demons don't stay dead, after all."

Christian looked with some sympathy at his naïve but well-intentioned protégé.

"Consider well the work we have done for Apollyon, my friend," he said. "I know firsthand that no real good ever comes from bargaining with such as him. He might spare our lives because we are still useful, but it would be a living death, and far worse for our families."

Christian looked at the morbid scene of death around him. He breathed in deeply and let the air out after holding it several beats.

"No," he continued, "if there is hope or mercy to be found now it certainly will not come from *his* kind. We are now enemies to Apollyon and there can be no bargaining. It is best to accept this as truth, and quickly."

He detected a slight slump of Faithful's shoulders as the ever-increasing reality of their situation added new burdens to his conscience. Christian was about to add another.

"Come, Faithful. We must get on."

"What about these poor souls?"

Christian knew what respect Faithful wanted to bestow on the slain and his heart ached a little as he laid the burden upon his friend, especially in light of what they had witnessed two nights prior. "Not this time. We must leave them for the sake of haste. 'Flee.' That is what the Evangelist commended us to do with his dying breath. Would this follower of Yeshua have said different? Come, now." Christian gently pulled Faithful's arm.

"Where are we going?"

Christian squinted into the morning sun over his shoulder. "To see an old friend, I hope. This way." He turned and trusted Faithful to follow as he began walking.

"But that is east," the young man said from behind him.

"I know."

"But won't this take us into—"

"—the Black Wood. I know."

"Have you ever been in the Black Wood?"

Christian walked back the several strides he had already taken and, when he was within reach, took the Book from its wedged space between the sheath of Faithful's sword and his armor.

"You are not my first friend to be swayed by this Book. We must go see another."

Faithful pondered this new information for a moment but did not look satisfied that Christian had addressed his concerns about the Black Wood. "OK. So we are going *east*."

Christian grinned at Faithful's apparent inability to grasp that they were about to go far into a direction which he had never been in his short life, and into a landmark about which he likely had heard one too many fireside stories.

"Yes, we head east. And our destination is the Black Wood."

Faithful took back the Book and both men returned to their original spot to retrieve their packs, and then they set off with brisk steps.

Away from Apollyon.

Away from Destruction.

CHAPTER EIGHT

Christian had never personally encountered the unique challenges of the Black Wood for he had never traversed *through* the old woodland. Several past adventures had taken him to the outlying parts of the forest, but he was never the leader of those parties. Under only the direst of circumstances, Christian had been warned by other Tracers, should one attempt to navigate into the Black Wood. Inside lay swamps, pits, dangerous carnivores, and worse if the rumors were to be believed.

Unfortunately, their new destination lay just east of the Black Wood and Christian and Faithful could not spare the time it would take to travel around the wood by common roads. Not with demonkind on their trail. No matter their road the Tracers were in danger, so if there was any chance that the Black Wood could expedite their journey, Christian decided that it was probably worth the risk. After all, the men could hardly be worse off than they already were as fugitive demon slayers.

Twilight was well upon them and there was still about a mile to go to the border of the Black Wood. With no guarantee of a moon and vivid recollections of their encounter with Apollyon, the Tracers set off at a run to reach their destination before nightfall, hoping that the denser wood might provide added cover from prying eyes. As they crested a hill, the Black Wood loomed before them, adding even more swiftness to their feet.

They entered the forest at full flight and the terrain turned down immediately. The momentum increased their pace to breakneck speed. Their feet found little traction on the layer of needles and packed dirt as they did their best to avoid rocks and tree trunks. Within minutes, as the decline steepened, their running became more and more like tumbling.

Faithful went down first. The crash stole Christian's attention as he saw his friend careening on his backside along a course off to Christian's side.

Even with his eyes fully engaged on his own situation Christian would have missed a root coming fast and sticking up just barely above the surface. The toe of Christian's book hooked it, pitching him forward into a roll that turned violent. He felt himself go over a small cliff and land again far enough below to knock the wind out of him.

It took only a moment for the shooting stars to clear from his eyes, but it would be several minutes before the rest of his body was ready to move. Nearby he could hear Faithful struggling and spitting the dust out of his mouth. Their packs were still securely fastened to their bodies, which had prevented their blades from coming loose or flying from their sheaths, but Christian again regretted his decision to pack his helmet away as he lay painfully on top of it. Christian also became aware of cold moisture seeping through his breeches, and less than a second later an aggravated groan from Faithful, followed by a disgusted "Blech!" confirmed that he must be experiencing the same thing.

Christian sat up and found that he was sitting just under the edge of a small cliff in the filthiest swamp he had ever seen...or smelled. The cliff ledge continued along to the north and south as far as he could see, and the swamp continued as far as he could see to the east—the direction they intended to travel.

"I think we're going to have to go through this," Christian said with a furled brow.

"Why not look for a way out?" asked Faithful.

"We can't spare the time traveling out of our way looking for an alternate route when it doesn't look as though there are any nearby."

Faithful studied the cliff ledge to the north and south until he must have come to the same conclusion. His response teetered on exasperation. "How did we miss this? It *stinks*! We should have smelled it a mile off!"

Christian nodded. "We must continue eastward, and this grimy slough has spoiled our torches. At least we'll be more difficult to spot without them, and our pursuers will not likely expect us to travel through such a swamp."

The initial excursion into the swamp was not too difficult at first. For a few hours the swamp rarely rose beyond their shins. But the incessant reek of mud and mold was taxing, if not downright sickening in spots. But as the night passed on, the mire came to engulf their thighs more and more often. Their only rest came from the handful of tiny islands they happened upon every so often with remnants of dead trees emerging from somewhat solid ground that they could lean on—some were even big enough to sit on for a longer break.

Even though their bodies were marginally strengthened by the occasional rest, their minds were restless with the memories of the campaign, the dying Evangelist's exhortations, and more immediate thoughts of what might be waiting for them in the deeper parts of the swamp. Fortunately, there was no sign of any demonic pursuers.

Onward they pushed through the night and into morning. In the new light, the Tracers could still see no end in sight—no dry land in any direction—and so the day seemed even more hopeless than the previous night.

The men were covered head to toe in the slimy soup, thanks to a couple of ill-fated steps each. They remained close for moral support as well as physical, but Faithful was having more difficulty dealing with the physical anguish that accompanied their predicament. Being his first wilderness campaign, his shoulders had not quite grown accustomed to carrying the weight of his armor, sword, and pack for long sustained periods over uneven ground, especially after the flight over the last mile to reach the forest. The lack of sleep was also increasingly wearying to both men.

By late morning it was common to be waist-deep in the swamp, having to fight harder for each new step that put increased strain on joints that were not used to the sucking downward pull of the mud. Faithful had added a desperate groan to his last dozen or so paces that concerned Christian with each utterance.

Christian also noticed that each of Faithful's steps took the young man farther from him. Weariness was setting in and Faithful could no longer navigate properly through his grogginess, and he now appeared to be heading into a deeper area of the swamp. Christian called out to his friend to halt, which he did, and Christian moved toward Faithful until he was beside him.

"We've got to head back to the shallower depths, Faithful," said Christian with genuine concern.

"I can't...I can't do this anymore."

Christian felt his heart ache as if the man were his own brother. He was so used to Faithful's inner strength that he had no idea how to handle this uncharacteristic resignation of defeat.

Faithful waivered, causing Christian to reach out to support him. The moment his fingers touched his companion's arm, Faithful leaned heavily against his mentor.

"I promised your father I would take care of you," Christian said. "I'm not going to let you die in this filthy swamp."

"My father...?" Faithful muttered, near delirium.

Christian quickly assessed that remaining immobile would certainly lead to a terrible end as the men would likely sink so far into the mud that they would become stuck, and Christian believed that it was unlikely he would find any kind of sure footing, preventing him from pulling his friend back to a relatively safe area. Christian unfastened the stopper of his water skin and poured some water down his throat before doing the same for Faithful. The cool moisture had some reviving effect on the men, though not as much as Christian had hoped. There was only one other option for easing their burdens.

"Turn around," Christian requested. Faithful half obliged, and Christian took a short step to face Faithful's back. He opened Faithful's pack and removed his helmet.

"I guess you won't need this anymore," he said as Faithful's heavy steel helmet hit the muck with a dull thud. While it slowly sank out of sight, Christian began removing all of Faithful's steel armor, and then he removed his own. Lastly, Christian turned Faithful back toward the east, the direction they would need to go, and turned his back to his friend.

"I don't need my helmet either."

As Faithful removed Christian's helmet from his pack, Christian thought of his last moments with Christy, when she had brought him his helmet and clung to it. He also thought of his children, who were frightened by the helmet and what it represented. He would be glad to be rid of it.

Christian turned to face Faithful as his own helmet hit the mud with a splat. Both men smiled and the effects of their lightened loads were immediate.

"We must continue forward," Christian urged. "Lean on me. One step at a time."

Faithful responded by simply carrying out the request, and the first step began the turn. Four more had them facing east.

"One at a time now," Christian repeated. It felt like ages had passed by the time the sludge was below their waists again.

Two paces to the right and they were on their way, moving faster than before with greater strength, bonded as one for the duration of the day's exhausting journey.

It was late in the afternoon when the men sighted the edge of the swamp, and well into dusk when they reached it. There was no strength for emotions like joy, and barely enough to even set their arms and heads upon the firm ground. Exhausted sleep threatened to overcome the men in spite of the fact that they were still half-submerged in the murky water.

"Save...yourself," came Faithful's weak attempt at something defiant.

"No," Christian responded with equal weakness. "I...I'll find something to pull us out."

Unfortunately, there was no root or low-hanging branch in sight. Christian was crest-fallen. They had slogged through this despicable mire only to be thwarted when they were so very near victory. Christian was contemplating the use of his sword: if he could just sink it deep enough into solid ground to pull himself out, if he removed his pack he might just have enough strength...

Faithful had another strategy.

"Yeshua... *help* us...!" he uttered.

Christian wasn't sure whether he should be amused or saddened by Faithful's desperate last resort—

"Hello there," greeted a deep voice from above.

His mouth agape, Christian looked up to where the friendly voice had come from and saw a young man (apparently not much older than Faithful) standing on the edge of the swamp in a long jade-green robe. He could barely make out the face as he seemed to be standing just perfectly in front of the sun (except the sun was to their backs, due to their eastward course)—in fact the "sunlight" edged the entire living form in brilliant gold.

The tall, strong man knelt down and studied the two Tracers curiously for a moment.

"What are you doing in the swamp?" he asked, his voice sounding like it was accompanied by distant chimes. Christian believed that his exhaustion was responsible for these oddities. He shook his head with what little energy he had left, convinced he had entered into a state in which he was unable to distinguish fantasy from reality. Neither he nor Faithful took the opportunity to answer the man's question.

A hand from the stranger was thrust toward Faithful and the man pulled him from the filth. Then the hand was offered to Christian. Upon gripping it, Christian felt as though some of his own strength was renewed.

"Thank you," said Faithful nearby, who—like Christian—was on his hands and knees catching his breath and covered in a layer of grime, but otherwise looking little worse for wear. "I feared this would be our grave," he added.

"Indeed, your fear would have served you better before entering this place. It can only be navigated at specific points by experienced guides."

"Why not simply build a way over this stinking bog if you locals know it's so dangerous?" Christian asked.

"There are straight paths of stone steps built and maintained as decreed by the King," the voice returned evenly. "But they are mostly hidden by the ever-flowing muck—certainly to anyone trying to start across in *darkness*. Still, take comfort that once immersed in its depths, you were both right to continue on your way and to seek someone to help you from this swamp. For it is the only way until His Majesty returns and dams up the flow of mud for good. But next time, *use the road*."

Christian almost laughed as he looked up and for the first time perceived that the cloaked figure was looking directly at him with purpose. Christian *felt* the man's eyes more than he saw them, but when their eyes connected Christian felt almost as though the man was looking into his very soul. He deflected his eyes to their surroundings as if searching for the path in question.

"Road? We'll try to remember that next time." Christian looked back at the man—but he was gone! "What the...?"

"Where did he go?" Faithful exhaled in utter bafflement. "One minute he was there and the next...nothing!"

The last thing Christian needed was another vision. "Our exhaustion... He couldn't have just vanished."

Faithful let the matter drop, and Christian couldn't help but reflect on how he felt when he met the man's gaze. A feeling of shame welled up as Christian considered how he had willingly donned the mark of Apollyon for so many years. He didn't know why, but somehow the way the enigmatic man had looked at Christian seemed to be the source of this newfound guilt. Or maybe it was all the long-repressed memories that this ordeal kept bringing to the forefront of Christian's mind...or his ever-present fear for his family's safety. He had seen the same penetrating look in the eyes of the dying Evangelist, so perhaps the guilt he now felt was a delayed effect of that encounter. Christian's world was quickly changing, once again, and he was now second-guessing every decision he had ever made.

Did these followers of Yeshua truly deserve their fate as sacrifices to Apollyon? Did *anyone* deserve to die for *any* reason in such a hopeless and humiliating manner? Was Apollyon the true rebel? Was Christian, and not these Evangelists, truly a rebel?

Christian shook the debate from his head. The Tracers had no more time to linger. As he stood on his feet, tendons and bones popped from the abuse they had been put through and his back stiffened beneath the weight of his remaining possessions, but he was unwilling to travel any lighter. All that remained of the men's armor were their leather breastplates, and they were not heavy enough to be worth compromising their safety any further. He certainly would not part with his sword.

Christian and Faithful drank some water and ate a quick meal from their soggy packs, and then set out with very little daylight remaining.

Beyond the swamp, the Black Wood was a mix of archaic beauty and heavy atmosphere. Just enough of the sky could be seen through the canopy above to keep their nerves steady, but only *just*. It appeared that all the trees had spent their centuries twisting themselves into strange wooden sculptures. The light and shadow played tricks on Christian's eyes, showing him "faces" or movement just enough at the periphery of his vision to make him doubt he had actually seen anything—except that this certainly occurred too frequently to be mere ghosts of his own imagining.

Behind him, Faithful had taken to using the final moments of daylight to read from the Book in search of anything that might help them in their travels, which was impressive as he still managed to navigate the forest without stumbling.

"So this is what the Evangelist meant..." he mumbled.

"Wha—?" said Christian.

"...'the wrath to come' that he spoke of. He was referring to—"

"—the Day of Judgment: when Yeshua's people believe that He will finally cast Apollyon, Apollyon's Fallen brothers, and all His enemies into the fire for eternal destruction. Quite the bedtime story, eh?"

"You've heard of this before?" said Faithful, amazed.

Christian let out an incredulous sigh. "It's nothing new. It's all the Evangelists talk about."

"Then you don't believe it?"

"I believe in the wrath of the past; failures and wayward acts against our fellow man, nature, and the powers of this world that build one upon one another like black monuments. I believe that as long as we don't appease the hunger of Apollyon and his demon hordes, they will make good on their promise to feed on everyone we love. I've seen it before and I would feed those monsters countless strangers before watching them devour everyone I love. But that is no longer an option for us now..." Christian trailed off, allowing a measure of the accusing guilt he felt toward Faithful to come through his voice.

"So it doesn't matter if we are no longer carrying out the duties of Apollyon? The King that this Book and the Evangelist speak about will not consider a pardon for us if we ask Him?"

"After the number of His followers we helped kill? What King would be so merciful? Would you be if you were in His place? Just remember that this King— Yeshua—is the Son of El Shaddai, who is the One who sets up Laws that no one can follow and then condemns them for breaking even one—*one time*. This means that to Him, we are no better than the Fallen and all their servants. At least *they* empower us to provide for our families and fight back against El Shaddai and his tyrannical Law—a Law He chooses to impose on those who do not wish to subscribe to it!"

"Based on the words of the Evangelist, it would seem that He would have the right to apply His Law to us all. Remember that He called *us* the rebels, and Belial and the others the *enemy*?"

"Of course he did," Christian spat back, hiding his inner doubts. "Doesn't every side think they are the right side?"

Faithful was silent, likely thinking up some new question to challenge Christian's experience.

And sure enough: "So if there is no hope for us, what good would it have been for the Evangelist to endure his suffering a little while longer to warn us? Why should he commend us to Yeshua and speak as if we could be part of His Kingdom, if He was as merciless as Apollyon would have been to us?"

"How should I know? Perhaps it amused him. Perhaps he thought it fitting punishment to give us false hope as recompense for handing his brothers and sisters over to Belial. I cannot say I would not have been tempted to do the same. Pretty shrewd, really."

Faithful was silent again, this time for so many minutes that Christian looked over his shoulder to see if he was still following. He saw his friend craning his neck to read the Book with the last rays of the day and then he turned his returned his gaze forward and sighed deeply: the conversation would go on. Christian thanked the heavens that the quiet reprieve lasted until the orange glow of the sky was nearly replaced by many shades of blue.

Faithful closed the Book and walked up beside Christian. "So you think the Evangelists and all the followers of Yeshua believe themselves to be perfect in keeping the Law?"

"They must if they believe themselves to be right with El Shaddai, though I don't see how they could believe that. They usually have an air of arrogant piety about them. Why else strut around so defiantly? The Evangelists we encountered must have believed their side to have adequate defenses against Belial and his brothers."

"Christian, this Book says that though we have broken the Law of El Shaddai, we are saved from El Shaddai's just wrath because Yeshua has made an atonement of blood for all His followers!"

Christian stopped cold and if the young man had been holding the Book (it was now tucked in his belt) he would have slapped it out of his hand clear to the horizon.

"You appear quick to accept every word in that Book," he chastised. Faithful ignored Christian's spite.

"The Book says that Yeshua was killed and raised to life again. All who believe in Yeshua are saved from the wrath to come. The Evangelist confirmed the words written here: all Yeshua's followers are given new lives in His Kingdom forever—deathless lives."

"It sounds like a fairy tale," was all Christian cared to reply.

Faithful looked at Christian with a sincerity that made him uncomfortable.

"Do you fear death?" Faithful asked.

Christian was almost surprised: finally a worthy question. "I care nothing for my own life. But I will *not* allow my family to be harmed."

Faithful considered this for a moment before responding.

"The Evangelist wasn't afraid to die either," Faithful said evenly. "In fact, he seemed almost glad, as if he were going home. Would he endure such a gruesome end for a dead King, Christian? What about the thousands of other

71

followers? What about those who wrote in this Book that they *saw* Yeshua life-less and buried in a tomb, only for Him to appear to them—and dozens of others too—*alive* just a few days later—*as flesh and blood*, bearing the marks of His death?"

"Did you see the Evangelist raised to life again?" Christian asked.

"Well, no" replied Faithful. "Perhaps that comes later."

Christian blinked, and blinked again. "Faith can be a powerful tool...or a wall to hide behind."

Faithful locked eyes with Christian. "You do not know these people beyond the tip of your blade, Christian. Neither of us does. We take their lives so that we might live. Yeshua *gave* His life so that others might live forever. He paid a debt He did not owe."

Suddenly the images of the fire consuming the neighbor family (and their estate) in Destruction, who had been found to be followers of Yeshua, flashed through Christian's mind. He had known the family well enough to testify that they had been good neighbors...peaceful and kind. They simply refused to serve Apollyon. The surrounding cottages had not been implicated with that family. But Apollyon's men had torched them anyway as a warning to the rest of the villagers. Had that truly been an act of good order by a just authority? And what about the atrocities he had seen during the Great Rebellion? Christian had to acknowledge that there was clearly a difference in the value that Apollyon and his rival, Yeshua, placed upon human life. And Faithful's father was a good man, though he was a rebel. Did he deserve his fate? Christian briefly wondered if he should tell Faithful of his father's conversion, but decided against it. Christian could not allow the legacy of Faithful's father to sway the young man's decision to follow Yeshua into an even more dangerous life.

The memories faded, bringing their surroundings into focus. The night had begun. The trees were different: fuller, younger, rich with life...

"I recognize this place... We have come through the Black Wood. We're close—"

A black spear rudely zinged over Christian's head.

"Demons!" cried Faithful, pointing through a cluster of tall trees.

72

"*RUN!*" Christian bellowed. He took off a little to the south, Faithful right beside him, with their opponents over fifty paces away (there were at least two based on the sound of the bellowing). The weight of their packs slowed them slightly as the chains threatened to chafe painful marks on their bodies. Fortunately, since they were still in the forest, speed was not as necessary to their escape while trees could provide some cover.

A spear splintered a tree just in front of them and began to smolder. Christian reflexively veered to the east and maintained his course at a good pace as he weaved among the large trunks, with Faithful keeping up admirably. A bestial roar erupted past them, confirming that their attackers were indeed demonkind. It was barely an hour into the night so it was likely the fiends had not yet fed. This made them dangerous but not quite as formidable.

The trees became sparse the further they progressed and the sound of rushing water could be heard in the near distance, getting closer as they scrambled through some brush.

When they emerged from the line of undergrowth they were upon a modest embankment edged with scatterings of rocks and foliage. A small river greeted them at the bottom that was about the width of three tall men laying head-to-foot. It flowed to the south, yet nearby it bent toward them in such a way that it would place Christian and Faithful on a course back to the east if they followed against its peaceful current. Christian had anticipated this and was glad his recollection of the area had placed them almost exactly where he had hoped. They thumped down the slope, and then shifted their path so that they ran against the river. The terrain began to roll slightly, enough that it did their lungs no favors, and the rushing din of water grew ever louder.

The Tracers passed through a natural arch of rock and earth and the terrain leveled out immediately. Before their eyes, at a far height above them, a waterfall tumbled gracefully into a pool about twice as wide as the river into which it was connected.

"Into the pool!" Christian exclaimed. He glanced over his shoulder to make sure his friend was following and found Faithful approaching apprehensively. "Trust me!"

73

"Wait a moment..."

"What?"

"A voice... I hear a voice above us. It's singing the most beautiful melody..."

Christian could not believe that he halted his own breathing to hear what his friend apparently heard. And indeed there was a sound with a musical quality to it, but if there were words they were not spoken in any language Christian had ever heard. "I hear nonsense. C'mon—"

"No, wait...!"

"We have no time, Faithful!" Christian added with desperate urgency. He did not know if it was his words or the spear that shattered nearby rocks that moved Faithful—Christian didn't care—soon after his companion was diving into the pool after him.

Beneath the water, everything was fairly illuminated by the moonlight reflecting off of the rocks below. The pack felt like a pillow on Christian's back after days of continuous wear. On the surface of the water, a thick layer of ice formed as the demons approached and drew all the nearby heat into their fiery cores. Christian expected this and knew that the demons would be furious at such an escape. He motioned to a short tunnel that was part of the rock face from which the water poured above. They passed through it and then swam up to the surface on the other side.

Christian and Faithful were now in a cave the size of a large room. A gentle breeze flowed in to them from the cave's mouth just as a terrible shriek of anger echoed from the cave wall behind them. A brash smile flicked across Christian's face, and Faithful added one of his own.

"They hate it when I do that," Christian said. Then he indicated the opening. "After you."

They pulled themselves out of the water and found their way out of the cave.

Outside the cave, which was carved into the side of a very steep hill, Christian stopped and let Faithful take in the impressive view. Painted in the silver sheen of the bright moon was a crater-like valley surrounded by steep cliffs that had the effect of high stone walls. Christian knew that the walls were equally as impassable (to human or demon) on the far side, providing this sanctuary with

74

great protection from demonkind. Within the green valley was a cornfield where gusts of wind could be seen running long sweeping fingers through its tall stalks. Directly at the center of the field was a small, stone house and barn.

Christian stepped into the field, intent on heading toward the house, but he stopped after about thirty steps. Someone else was in the field nearby. The clear squeaking of a lantern could be heard and it was coming toward them quickly. Christian drew his sword, less because he expected a threat and more because he did not know what kind of reception he would receive.

The sound of the swaying lantern stopped. "Who goes there?" The voice was well-worn, but it was strong and carried with it the promise of a good fight should it be underestimated.

Christian and Faithful held their breaths. Christian wasn't sure how to respond. He had come here for help on behalf of their families, but he was no longer sure that he would be welcome.

"Oh, you're no demons."

Christian snapped his head to the right where a rebellious-looking older man, with wild white hair and powerful eyes, had silently stepped through the corn toward the men.

"Get a lot of demon visitors here, old man?" Christian replied.

"Ha! You would think they should know better but they always like to try." The elder gentleman raised the lantern to get a better look at the two fugitives. "Christian my friend, is that you?"

CHAPTER NINE

Christian and Faithful sat at a long wooden table, drying themselves in the warmth of the large fire in the hearth. The house of the old man was simple but tidy. In the corner of the main living area, on a wooden perch, was a one-eyed falcon that had seen better days. A single bed rested in the corner under a loft with two more beds that could only be reached by a rickety ladder. Everywhere else—surface, floor, shelf, and nook—were books and rolls of parchment.

At the table, Faithful was again lost in the pages of his Book. Meanwhile the old man was scooping hot stew from a pot over the fire into two large bowls. Faithful paused and examined the fire with apprehension.

"Is that safe?" Faithful asked his host.

"Your friend here has never complained about my cooking," the elder laughed.

"I mean the fire," Faithful clarified.

"Why wouldn't it be?"

"Demons use fire as a…doorway," Faithful continued, looking as though he felt a little foolish saying it out loud for the first time and wondering how this man might not know this.

"My word, young man! This fire has never been so defiled. It is protected."

"Protected?" Faithful asked.

Their host removed the cooking pot from the fire and Faithful could see, carefully inscribed in the stone of the fireplace, a message:

GREATER IS HE WHO IS IN YOU THAN HE WHO IS IN THE WORLD

Interpreter studied Faithful's expression for a long moment before returning the pot to the fire. "They are words from The Book," said Interpreter, pointing to Faithful's Book on the table. "The King's Words are life."

"You are sure that works?" Christian asked with skepticism.

"I'm alive, aren't I?" the man retorted.

"Now you see why our friend is called the Interpreter," Christian said to Faithful with a smile. "He's always been smarter than most."

Interpreter chuckled. "Smarter than *some,* anyway. And I'm sorry young man; I didn't catch your name."

"Faithful, sir," he replied.

"Ah, Faithful..." Interpreter's eyes widened as he made the connection and his attention shot to Christian. Christian nodded in silent confirmation to his elder. "Nice to meet you."

Faithful smiled.

When Interpreter was satisfied that the meal was in order, the Tracers' host placed the steaming bowls of stew before his guests, and then he took a place at the table opposite them. Faithful closed the Book and pushed it aside to eat, his eyes trained on the old man, who smiled warmly and understood that Faithful was not just hungry for food.

"How do you know Christian?" Faithful inquired eagerly. "Did you used to patrol together?"

The elder chap gave a curious look to Christian. "Oh we used to do more than that, young man. We fought together in the Great Rebellion—or at least that's what we called it back then. He was my best pupil in those raids against demonkind."

Faithful's eyes widened. "So you knew my father?" he asked excitedly through a mouthful of stew.

The elder man gave Christian another curious look, this one with a hint of confusion.

"Of course I knew your father! He was a great man, and one does not easily forget great men, especially when they bring him news of Yeshua the King."

Faithful took several moments to process the new information. "Wait," he finally asked in amazement, "my father told *you* about Yeshua?"

Interpreter nodded. "I've been following the True King since the day your father was killed."

Faithful stood in anger and addressed Christian. "You never told me that my father was an Evangelist!"

"I was trying to keep you and your mother safe," Christian said calmly, remaining in his seat. Faithful was silent for another moment and then sat back down.

"Mother never told me either," he said.

"Your mother never knew," said Christian, and Faithful's face reddened again.

"You kept it from her as well? My father kept it from us?"

"Your father didn't keep anything from you," Christian said, knowing that he was about to incur further wrath. "He was converted during our last campaign and killed before he had the chance to share the news with you and your mother. After his death, his personal beliefs seemed less important than your safety."

"You had no right!" erupted Faithful.

"Now, now," Interpreter chimed in. "Do go easy on him, young man. Christian saved your life after all, and your mother's."

"What do you mean?" Faithful asked.

Christian lurched out a hand, clasping Interpreter's forearm as an unspoken warning not to proceed.

The elder's eyebrows creased together, as if violated by the manner of the sudden gesture. "He has a right to know," he said.

"Know what?" Faithful was now exasperated.

"Be patient young man, and I will tell you. Our Great Rebellion was not about Yeshua or El Shaddai—nothing of the sort. It was about *liberty*. We were tired of living under the thumb of Apollyon and fighting his battles. Your father and I were once Tracers together. We built support among others in Apollyon's ranks, and some from the outside, like Christian. Christian was a young man in those days—a farmer, in fact—but he became our greatest pupil and a fierce demon slayer. After all, it was *he* who discovered their weakness—their eyes!"

Faithful looked at Christian in awe, then returned his gaze to Interpreter.

"Unfortunately," Interpreter continued, "our rebellion would not last. I don't know all the details about how it happened, but before our final battle against Apollyon's forces, your father had changed. He spoke of redemption, salvation, and eternal life. His death…the way he died…" Interpreter choked up with emotion and decided to expedite his explanation. "Your father's death was a strong testimony to me of the power of faith in Yeshua, and I decided that day to follow Him."

Interpreter took a moment to regain his composure and Christian decided that he might as well continue the story. "Most of our forces were gathered when our families were brought, bound and battered, out to the battle field. They were slaughtered before our very eyes. Naturally, it was more than most could bear.

"I had to get to them…" Interpreter continued. "I had to get to my family. Noble Christian here was the last holdout and notorious among demonkind—feared even. He had no family of his own but decided to surrender in order to buy me time to reach my family. He had only one condition, when presented before Apollyon himself: the lives of you and your mother. Much to everyone's surprise, Apollyon agreed, and Christian entered into Apollyon's service that very day."

For many minutes only the crackling of the fire could be heard.

It was Faithful who broke the silence. "You made a deal with the devil," Faithful said to Christian, "to save us?"

Christian remained still and felt awkward at so much attention being given his past deeds, for which he himself felt mostly shame. He finally turned to Interpreter.

"Did they make it?" He asked. "Your family—I must know!"

Interpreter studied Christian, and then deduced, "You have a family of your own."

Christian's eyes filled with tears. "I must help them. I must save them."

"We are now fugitives," Faithful cut in, seeing the difficulty that Christian had in continuing.

"My family is safe in Celestial City, as it is with so many others whose faith through trial is rewarded."

"*The* Celestial City?" Faithful responded eagerly.

The Interpreter pointed to the closed Book that the young man was holding so tightly. "You'll read all about it in there. It's the King's city, Yeshua's Kingdom where His followers live forever in immortal bodies. And when He returns this *whole world* will be remade just like it—*forever*."

Faithful played a fingernail along the wood grain of the table. "It seems too easy to just follow Yeshua, and so hard to believe anyone can truly conquer death and live."

"Indeed, because we are surrounded by death and those who love darkness more than light, the Truth can seem like foolishness. Our cursed natures believe the darkness will hide our wickedness and shame. Many accept this lie. Others are tempted to think that they can win the favor of El Shaddai by keeping His Law. They often dream of great rewards and riches if they can merit His favor by keeping His commands. Yet it is simply the will of El Shaddai that we seek out and give our allegiance to His Son.

The atmosphere in the room became contemplative for a moment. Then Faithful said softly, "I see now that I am not worthy in myself of El Shaddai's great mercy, but it makes my heart leap for joy that He would provide eternal life in His Kingdom of Celestial City through His Son's sacrifice. I see that I am not my own and have been granted freedom from my prison of spiritual debt by the Atonement of Yeshua. Out of thankfulness for His sacrifice of blood, I will follow Him—if He will have me."

Interpreter's eyes glistened. "You are truly your father's son, and Yeshua will have you indeed! Because He lives you will live also."

"Have you seen Him?" Faithful asked. "Have you seen Yeshua the King?"

Interpreter nodded. "Oh yes, Faithful, I have seen Yeshua. Death holds no sway over Him and neither will it conquer you while you cling to Him."

Christian swallowed the lump of anger welling in his throat. "If Yeshua were truly alive why does He do *nothing* while we live and die as slaves to Apollyon and his demon hordes?"

"*Nothing*? He sends Evangelists to bring you word of the coming final Judgment! They bring you *that Book*!"

"I don't understand..." said Faithful.

Interpreter looked at the young man. "Like those who wrote the words in that sacred tome, the Evangelists give their lives in the most brutal ways to bring you, those you love, and your neighbors the Good News and word of the King's imminent coming. We will never know exactly what hour He will come, only that He will. 'Soon,' He said 'soon.' Everything you need to know is in that Book. Trust in it. Trust in the true King. That is where you will find your strength to press on toward the goal, as they do—as *I* do.

"Trust in a King who keeps you *here* and not with your family?" Christian asked.

"There is still work to be done. Until He summons me to the great gates of Celestial City I am in His service in this world, offering sanctuary and guidance to pilgrims such as you."

"You're telling me to have faith?" Christian scoffed.

The elder nodded.

Christian sank his head into his hands, contemplating that word: faith. The war in his mind raged full-force and the images of his nightmare-vision threatened to engulf him in unbridled fear. But he could no longer stand to watch those for whom he cared so deeply be taken from him. His family had nearly perished with those neighbors who met their tragic fate in that hellish blaze and he had watched so many more suffer and die in his youth.

He had believed that becoming an elite Tracer for Apollyon would give him control over their fates, over his. He had thought that by helping to destroy Yeshua's followers that somehow Yeshua would either prove to be powerless, or be forced to come to their aid so that Christian could know His strength. He tried telling himself that Yeshua probably didn't even exist, though the proof was overwhelming. His fear had clouded everything—all his senses and reason. Faith

81

was for the pious. How could Yeshua ever receive him in His Kingdom when Christian had the blood of so many of His followers on his hands? Furthermore, his family had shared his fears and supported him, thus surely they were as good as condemned with him. *He had led his family in down the wrong path.* A terrible weight overcame him, like someone had tied an anvil to his back, and he nearly pitched forward by this new burden…but Interpreter's hand touched his shoulder and brought new hope to Christian's mind. Christian did not turn to face his elder, who remained behind him.

"Surely our families will be safe until we are captured...?" Christian asked hopefully.

"There are no guarantees," Interpreter answered. "I've been hearing rumors that Apollyon and his demonkind are behaving oddly; that they are becoming unpredictable."

"Have you many friends outside this sanctuary?" Christian asked.

"Suffice it to say that we Evangelists are a well-organized minority," Interpreter replied. "I get the information I need."

Christian nodded. "It would appear that you have heard correctly about Apollyon and his demons. They seem to be recruiting… What have I done?"

Interpreter turned Christian to face him. "You have done right to come here for help, to hear words of hope that you have not heard for far too long. Indeed, it is an answer to my prayer of so many years to see you here tonight. You are a good man, Christian, indeed one of the best. But that cannot save you or your family. You cannot save yourself."

Christian bowed his head. "Is there any hope for my family?"

Interpreter placed his hand on Christian's shoulder and stared deeply and compassionately into his friend's eyes. "There is always hope. It's not the King's will that any of His children should perish, and His power is great. Greater than you can ever imagine."

Christian thought again of the inscription from the fireplace, then again of his family. His shoulders slumped, feeling the imagined weight on his back match the level of brief comfort that Interpreter's words had given him. By his experience it was unlikely that the King could truly have any mercy for one such as him, but he would surely receive none returning to his duties under Apollyon. He was resigned to his fate at the hands of Yeshua.

"What must we do?"

"I can make the path clear, and then you must seek out the King to plead your case. And you must leave with all haste."

The old man suddenly walked to the fire. He took a handful of strange powder from a jar on the mantle and threw the fine grains into the hearth. Immediately a sharp scent of spice and herbs filled the air and a snow-white smoke filled with embers wafted up the chimney.

"What are you doing?" Christian exclaimed.

Interpreter was too busy placing foodstuffs and supplies into a pair of burlap sacks to answer. As he packed the gear, Christian and Faithful looked at each other.

The door opened behind them and through it entered a cloaked figure that Christian and Faithful immediately recognized: the man dressed in jade that had helped them from the swamp and just as abruptly left them.

"You...!" Christian exclaimed, instinctively reaching for his sword at the visitor's sudden arrival. Meanwhile Faithful flashed him a look of friendly rebuke.

"Gentlemen, gentlemen," said Interpreter, standing fast between the Tracers and the newcomer, "this is my loyal friend and guide on many bitter roads. He goes simply by the name of 'Help'. Even if he had another name I think I would ignore it, for Help could not be more fitting for him."

Help smiled at the Tracers while Christian looked to his former mentor to carry on.

The old man said, "He's the one I signaled through the fireplace just now. He will be going with me."

Christian's brow furrowed. "Going with you? Where?"

"To retrieve your families, of course."

"No, I will go myself!" Christian protested.

"You *cannot*. You must draw the demons away. Seek out the King and tell Him everything so that we may find success with His blessing."

Christian looked deeply into Interpreter's eyes. In his mind flashed the horrible vision of his family's destruction and their muted screams threatened to overwhelm his mind. He thought of the joy he found in playing with his children the night before his departure and Christy's fear for their safety. His family was counting on *him* to keep them safe and he couldn't fail them. Not again. A renewed sense of urgency quickened his pulse.

"Christian," Interpreter pleaded, "you once bought me the time necessary to save my family. I cannot do the same for you—I am of far less interest to demonkind than you are," Interpreter trailed off briefly. "Indeed, it seems that I am usually of less importance to their kind," he mumbled, reminiscing more to himself than to his company. "But let me help you, Christian. Let me retrieve your family while demon eyes are upon you."

Christian stared deeply into his old friend's eyes and studied him for a long moment. "Very well, I will seek out the King and beg for His mercy on my family—our families," Christian added with a nod to Faithful, "and on each of us. I will never again lead my family down the wrong path, and if Yeshua is the answer as you claim, I will accept His instruction and offer him my sword."

Though he trusted Interpreter, Christian couldn't help but reflect for one last moment on the notion that he wouldn't be the one to retrieve his family. His fear took hold and he felt his knees buckle as again sweet memories of the past joined his horrific nightmare vision of the possible future, engulfing him in despair. "I can't lose them."

Interpreter got on his knees in front of Christian as a father might approach to console his son. "There there, fear not. I will set out this very hour to retrieve your families. My friend and I will travel night and day. I will bring them to this sanctuary until I receive further instruction."

Christian thought of the high surrounding cliffs, limited access, and protected fireplace. He finally felt at least a small amount of relief.

"Thank you. Thank you, my friend!"

Interpreter rose back to his feet, pulling Christian gently with him. "Come now. You must both be off at once. There is no more time to spare." Interpreter handed a sack to Faithful as he opened the cottage door and moved to the front porch. Christian followed, took the sack that the old man held out for him and shouldered it as he joined his friend.

"Thank you, sir," Faithful added. "I now see why they call you the Interpreter, for you have made so many things clear to me."

The elder waved the pleasantry off good-naturedly. "Well, we must stick together after all. We 'rebels'…we pilgrims. Now go on."

Bearing torches in front and behind, respectively, Interpreter and Help led Christian and Faithful along a stone path to a high, fortified steel door set into the foot of the cliff wall bordering the eastern side of the estate. Inside the door was a short, slim wicket gate (or man-sized inset door), etched with another engraving that Christian presumed to be from the Book:

ASK AND IT WILL BE GIVEN TO YOU

SEEK AND YOU WILL FIND

KNOCK AND IT WILL BE OPENED TO YOU

"Remember this?" Christian's former mentor asked, indicating the small gateway.

Christian remembered it well, and the adventure they were on when they discovered it. He watched as his friend removed a large golden key from his pocket and unlocked the wicket gate for them. Despite its clearly archaic age, there was barely the slightest hint of a rusted squeak from its hinges as the gate swung toward them. Beyond was a long tunnel.

The elder turned to them. "This tunnel will take you under the mountain. Just outside you will cross a small stream, and on the other side of that stream you will come across a straight and Narrow Road. There is *none* like it in all the world. It is this Road, heading due east, that will take you to Celestial City by the design of El Shaddai and the work of Yeshua Himself. It is the only one that will do so! The Road won't always be easy, in fact it rarely is, but it is always clearly marked. Never lose sight of the Road, and never stray far from it, for there will be destruction and death all around you. Stay the course!"

Christian began to feel anxious, which puzzled him terribly. He could not remember ever feeling this apprehensive. Then again, he'd never been on a journey quite like this before.

"There are often Palaces along the Road designed to provide further instruction and encouragement from the Book that will be useful for your journey," Interpreter continued. "Those Palaces are refuges where you may receive many blessings to strengthen your spirits. Finally, you will also find that these sanctuaries will have the means to replenish your provisions and provide rest as needed. Never allow your pride to prevent you from receiving their charity, for you will likely regret it."

Christian looked down at his feet for several moments before he could muster the courage to look at Interpreter. "I have stared demonkind in the eye without the skip of a heartbeat, met their lords with a set jaw, traversed the streets of Mansoul, helped to take the lives of many men—deserved or not—without hesitation. I was Christian, the Great Rebel, and then I became known in the City of Destruction as one of the best of the Tracers employed by Apollyon. And yet I do not think I have the strength of faith you expect from me to make this journey, nor will I ever have it. What if the King will not help my family? What if harm comes to you all because of the evil I have done? What if in His just reason Yeshua will not show mercy to my wife and children—even if I were to give myself in their place? How will I even know He will hear my plea?"

This time it was Help who placed a confident hand on Christian's shoulder. "Yeshua was not sent into the world to condemn the world but to save it. He is very much alive and keen on reclaiming *all* creation as His own once more, so it will all be as Celestial City is now. He will make all things new."

Help paused for a beat or two, either to catch his breath or to see if there were any further questions. However, Interpreter allowed no time for new inquiries.

"My friends, it is time for us to part." He pushed the two men gently into the tunnel and then blocked the archway with his body. "Please ensure the entrance to this passage remains hidden on the far side. The enemy is always seeking entrance into the strongholds of the King's followers."

Interpreter suddenly disappeared for several moments. Then Christian and Faithful heard an "Ah, yes, of course!" but he remained out of sight for nearly a minute.

When the old man reappeared he was holding a pair of crimson traveling cloaks. "I forgot, but thankfully loyal Help did not." He handed them each a cloak that fastened together at the neck by a brooch of gold and ruby depicting a dove upon a triangle, and explained, "These are gifts from the King for travelers embarking on this difficult journey." Christian nodded after fastening his new cloak and managed a smile. "You are a true friend."

The door started to close as Christian and Faithful turned to proceed down the tunnel, which was illuminated only by the early dawn light coming through the opening at the far end.

They had not even gone ten steps when Interpreter suddenly called to them to halt for one last word: "Let your lives be a guide to your families. They will follow your path, so see to it that it remains on the straight and narrow. Godspeed, my friends!" The wicket gate closed, and both Christian and Faithful moved forward through the tunnel.

When they finally reached the other end, the men removed the underbrush blocking their exit and, once through, replaced the covering with the coming dawn giving aid to their new adventure.

"Here," Christian said, pulling Faithful close and loading his sack of supplies into the young man's traveling bag. Faithful, in turn, did the same for his companion.

"So it begins," the young man said. Christian smiled and placed a hand on his friend's shoulder.

Both men looked eastward along the Road they were bidden to walk, and stepped upon the Narrow Road.

CHAPTER TEN

John heard a commotion outside his cell door and rushed to hide the Book under the still body of his cellmate. Then he crossed the cell and leaned against the soiled stone wall as Despair worked the door latch. With John in full view of the Ogre, the door swung open and Despair's long silhouette cast itself into the cell like a dancing specter.

Despair held a tray with a measly selection of food—or at least what might have once been properly called "food". Despair suddenly lifted a stiff boot to John's ribs. Despite the lancing pain from the unprovoked abuse, John did not respond. He knew better than to do so; his screams would only give the Ogre satisfaction and the desire to repeat his unwarranted violence. It was best for him to see John as a boring, decrepit creature not worthy of his time.

"I brought extra for your friend," Despair growled.

John flicked his eyes to the tray and was subtly amused by what the Ogre defined as "extra". But otherwise he made no reaction or movement, lest the monster throw the pathetic meal to the ground in a tantrum and make it even less worthy of a starving mouth.

Despair looked at the newcomer.

"What's the matter? Ain't you hungry?" he bellowed.

When the unconscious man did not so much as twitch, the monster heaved the tray of stale bread and mushy gruel across the room against the farthest wall he could find. He watched the food move like snails racing down the face of the stone, and then burst out with a roar of his offensive laughter.

"Beast," John muttered.

The Ogre looked at him, but not because he had heard the utterance of his captive. "Been a while since you've had a friend, ay? Last one didn't last too long. Did 'e?"

"Monster," replied John, a little louder than his first retort. This time he was sure the Ogre had heard him.

Despair chuckled dangerously, then grabbed John by the head and threw him forward with enough momentum to send him headlong into the pile of gruel on the dirt floor, where roaches had already flocked en masse.

"Go on! Eat!" More maniacal laughter ensued as John quickly picked himself up off the floor and scooted on hands and knees back to a sitting position against the rough stone face.

The giant growled and kicked John hard against the stone wall, causing dirt and gravel to fall from the carved stone ceiling.

"Your loss!" Despair roared.

The cell door slammed shut, causing another cascade of earth. When the dust settled, the whole scene appeared the very definition of misery. John picked himself up with a pained grunt, dusted himself off, grabbed the tray, and proceeded to pick up the remnants of the rations—which meant hunting for the scattered bread and scraping what he could of the gruel off the rock and into the serving dish. At one point he needed to contend with a mangy (but plump) rat, which he got the better of by trapping it beneath a nearby bowl.

"I'll save *you* for later!" he exclaimed in victory.

John brought the putrid meal to his needy friend and placed some bits of gruel into the man's mouth with his fingers. The reaction from the exhausted soldier was as he expected—more coughing. When most of the man's coughing had subsided, John said, "Not hungry, eh? I suppose you can't even call this 'food'."

John put the tray down and instead reached for some water, which the man accepted gratefully. John's thoughts wandered, but to where he did not know for no images accompanied his daydream.

John shook his head and glanced at the man lying beside him, who had closed his eyes again and entered into a restless sleep. With a heavy sigh, John reached beneath the man for the Book and decided to read again from its printed pages, planning to continue with the journal portion later.

* * *

Hours later, Christian sat bolt upright with a gasp.

John dropped the Book with a start as Christian studied the scrawny, scraggily-bearded figure sitting before him.

Regaining his composure, John asked, "You... Are you okay now?" He then added something else in a whisper that was incoherent to Christian.

Christian looked around the room very much dazed from the manner in which he had awoken (with no help from his lack of real food).

"Where am I?" he asked.

"You're in a dungeon," replied John, exasperated by the daft question. "Doubting Castle specifically, if you want to send someone a letter."

Christian chuckled through his pain and looked at his cynical companion. "Why are we here?"

The man shrugged. "I'm not entirely sure, but I've come to think that we must be some kind of sad pets."

"Pets?" Christian winced as he moved to sit against the wall.

"Yes. The Ogre who keeps us here—"

Christian scowled at the word "Ogre".

"His name is Despair and he loves human suffering…if he can *love* anything at all. To him, suffering is good sport. My real curse, though, is not the Ogre so much as my talent for survival."

Christian rubbed his eyes with one hand. "I was hoping I had dreamt the part about the Ogre."

The scraggily man stood on his feet awkwardly and thrust out a bony hand. "I'm called John, by the way."

The former Tracer accepted the hand. "Christian."

John gave a short nod of the head. "Pleased to meet you, Christian."

90

Christian smiled and gave a quick nod in return. "John, may I please have some more water?" His cellmate complied and Christian thanked him.

John held up the Book. "Seems like you've had quite an adventure. Is this all true?"

"It's true," Christian replied, looking away.

"The front part's very difficult to make out. Too much blood."

Christian continued deflecting his gaze. "Yeah...well I'm afraid I'm partially to blame for that." He carefully slid up the wall and stood to his feet. Finding himself steady enough after letting the initial light-headedness pass, he walked along the wall, feeling his way around the cool, filthy stone with fingers searching for any sign of structural weakness.

"You're a hearty one," John said. "You look as though you've been trampled by a horse and buggy, and you've had nothin' but a few sips of brackish water. Are you sure you're well enough to be on your feet?"

Christian shrugged and threw a quick glance at John, whose gloomy expression reflected unease.

"I've had my share of knocks and bruises. This is nothing," said Christian. "My body should recover quickly enough once we get out of this stink hole."

The horrified look on John's face told Christian more about his new companion than words could have. He decided to make his intentions clear.

"I do not make a good 'pet', John."

"What do you expect to do? Escape?"

John had clearly understood Christian's intent. Christian hoped his silence would definitively settle the matter, but it only served to transition John's apprehension into full-on dismay.

"That's suicide! He'll never let you out!"

"The Ogre you mean?"

"No, that rat over there. Of course the Ogre!"

Christian halted his investigation and thought about whether or not he should press John's defeatist mind any further. He decided he should, because he wanted to help him.

"Is there only one?"

"Is one Ogre not enough?" John was quite maniacal now.

Christian stopped what he was doing entirely and turned to look directly at John. He was willing to chance that the Ogre had been horribly abusing John. After so many years of abuse and suppressed anger, Christian was more than confident there was a good deal of fight in John waiting to be unleashed. To the common eye he was a gaunt wisp of a creature, but Christian had been around enough men like him—both friend and foe—to appreciate just how strong and nimble such a man as John could be.

"Well, there are *two* of us," Christian finally answered.

John sighed. "As far as I know he's the only one. And I've been here a long time. A really long time."

John mumbled something else that sounded like it was the same thing as the last words, only with more emphasis. Then he sighed again and Christian knew that his new companion had accepted the scenario.

Christian turned his attention back to the walls. "Tell me about yourself, John."

"Not much to tell, really. I was born a subject of Apollyon and I'll die here in a failed escape attempt."

Christian tried not to laugh. Yes, he definitely liked this man and resolved to do all he could for him. "That can't be all there is to your story."

"Well, it's certainly not as interesting as yours." John bent down to retrieve the Book from where it had fallen, opened it up, and then closed it again as he dumped his frame onto the ground in a heap. After a few moments reflection, John said, "Well, my eyes need a break from this chicken scratch and you're full of youthful vigor. Why don't you entertain ol' mad John with more of your story?"

"Where did you leave off?" Christian asked.

"You and your younger companion were just embarking on the Narrow Road."

Christian smiled, nodded, and agreed to the request, even as he continued to assess their environment.

CHAPTER ELEVEN

Days and nights passed for Christian and Faithful as they sought Yeshua with single-minded determination. They no longer kept track of the days, though Christian figured it had been a month since he and his companion parted ways with the Interpreter. They stopped at nearly every Evangelist Palace they came across, although Christian was not yet comfortable entering.

"You need not trust in the King to find rest here, Christian," Faithful often told him. "They welcome any pilgrim in need of rest."

Christian made up an unconvincing excuse about not wanting the feel of a soft bed to make him forget the urgency of his mission, but in reality he was not comfortable taking advantage of the hospitality of such devoted followers of Yeshua when he himself was not convinced of this new King's immortality. The guilt and shame he felt over having been responsible for the deaths of so many Evangelists also prevented him from crossing any Palace threshold.

Christian did not prevent Faithful from enjoying the comforts that the Palaces had to offer and, though he slept alone outside, Christian graciously and thankfully accepted the provisions brought to him by Faithful's hosts.

Faithful, on the other hand, found his spiritual needs administered to precisely as the Interpreter said they would be. The pilgrims quickly learned that those allied with the demons had also built structures that resembled "Palaces" to lure unsuspecting pilgrims through lies and cunning philosophies. These false houses were usually set quite a distance from the Road and after a while Faithful found that he needed to question the hosts to be sure of their true nature. The caretakers of true Palaces never minded this inquiry and indeed welcomed the questions as a sign of "good spirit-testing faith".

Besides these infrequent reprieves at the Palaces, they stopped only to gather fruit or grain from the side of the Road, to drink from nearby streams, or to sleep just off the Road beside campfires so small that Christian was certain no demon could traverse them. They were always watchful for any sign of demonkind, but as of yet had not uncovered any evidence that they had been followed from Interpreter's valley sanctuary.

Faithful enjoyed reading from the Book, and along the Road they often met with a range of people, some genuine and others more devious. One person thought himself wise in the ways of the world, as evidenced by his vast wealth and certificates of education, while another boasted of his knowledge of the law and the ways it could save a man by looking to himself; a woman spoke proudly of her ability to find great meaning in culture and philosophy, and one young man was simply talkative for its own sake so as to prevent Christian or Faithful from getting in any word at all. At points these people made sense but in the end, as Faithful searched the Book to compare their words with the wisdom contained therein, he found that none were willing to bend a knee to Yeshua the King and he wondered why they were on the Narrow Road at all.

Indeed many took terrible offense when Faithful told them that they were the created design of El Shaddai, or that Yeshua had given Himself in Atonement for the rebellion of the world to save those who would believe and follow Him.

"I admire your persistence," Christian said, chuckling to Faithful after parting with one group of travelers under such circumstances.

"I pray for them," Faithful replied sincerely.

"I am sure that El Shaddai would much rather hear from you than me."

"I'm not better than you, Christian," said Faithful. "I pray that El Shaddai will reveal Himself to you in some way.

Christian knew that Faithful also prayed for him. It was harder for Christian to pray at all, though he sometimes tried—especially during the quiet moments before sleep when he most longed to see his family safe and reunited. Christian struggled with the persistent lack of any news regarding the well-being of his family. Didn't Yeshua have messengers? Couldn't He have appeared to them by now so that Christian could plead the case that weighed upon his heart, that they might yet be saved?

In spite of his anguish and frustration, Christian found some enjoyment in Faithful's enthusiasm and ability to use his Book to frustrate their occasional acquaintances, especially when the passers-by so often grew hostile when his friend only meant to bring them Good News. The Book itself also provided many words of comfort that Faithful would read aloud, but words alone meant less to Christian than meaningful action. Thus it was too often tempting to fall into depression or anger when he felt powerless. When Christian expressed these feelings to Faithful, his companion offered to pray with him or read something from the Book's Psalms.

Faithful tried to convince his friend that El Shaddai wanted to hear these things as much as praise and worship, just as any father desired to know the troubles of his children. While Christian wanted to believe this, he remained unconvinced. Christian's cynical heart beat unabated, and he suffered anxious nights as the vivid nightmares of his family's demise came close to breaking his tormented spirit.

* * *

Christian stared at the midday sun and wiped sweat from his brow as Faithful packed his Book in anticipation of the challenge before them: they had come to a fork in the Road and one path, the obvious continuation of the Narrow Road, rose very steeply up a rocky hill. From what they could see of the hill, a large swath of the southern face was a mess, as if a titan in some forgotten age had bashed a massive club across that side of the mound leaving a gaping, craggy cliff.

The other, easier-looking path lead around the foot of the hill to the north and could be seen curving, presumably back toward the Road on the other side of the hill, but it was beyond their view and impossible to confirm. A small clear spring lay just beyond the fork.

"Figures," said Faithful, surveying the challenge before them.

Christian agreed and breathed out an irritated sigh. "Yeah, this will be difficult."

95

The pilgrims walked to the spring, leaned down to clean their faces, and drank from the cool water. As Christian poured some water over his sun-browned neck, Faithful filled their water skins from the spring.

The sunlight dimmed as if a cloud had passed beneath the sun, but there had been no clouds when Christian gazed up at the sky minutes before. He turned his head in the direction from which they had come and found three women approaching from the north. They were exceedingly beautiful: none of the three were older than thirty, their bronze faces and necks were unadorned, and they were dressed immodestly in tattered old clothes (strangely unfitting for their beauty) that still managed to reveal the curvature of their feminine forms. Christian stood to face them.

Faithful, who had been mid-drink, turned his body to determine what could have taken his friend's attention from such refreshing pool. His gaze locked on the women.

Christian could tell that Faithful would not be speaking and chuckled to himself.

"Greetings pilgrims," the eldest of the young women said cordially. "How fare you?"

"Well enough, ma'am, thank you," Christian replied.

Christian waited to see what the women wanted. He had no desire for conversation that might delay his journey up the difficult hill.

"We're desperate, I'm afraid. Desperate," the same woman finally continued in a manner that sounded forced and disingenuous.

Christian sighed and turned his head to survey the hill. He felt a real sense of urgency to conquer the hill before sunset, knowing well that this difficult hill would prevent their flight in the event of a demon attack. He needed to find the King before it was too late for his family, and for weeks, with each passing day, he and Faithful could feel an increasing longing to reach Celestial City. He turned back to the three women. He was not unconcerned about whatever their plight might be, but something about this present situation seemed unsettling. Where had they come from?

"What seems to be the trouble?" he managed with as much sincerity as he could muster.

This time the youngest woman spoke. "Well you see, *the King* has stationed our father on the other side of this hill to give aid to passing pilgrims, only he's grown old and frail and cannot tend our fields. When pilgrims such as you come by, we've got nothing to offer."

The pouting tone that the youngest sister added to her words was almost too much for Christian to endure with a straight face. He was sure they were being cajoled by these women, and how convenient that their estate lay beyond view around the hill.

"We'll make do, thank you," Christian said with a polite smile.

"Surely your company is enough to offer any weary pilgrim," Faithful added. "Did you say you serve the King?"

Christian realized it had probably been a mistake not to intone haste in his voice for the sake of his entranced friend. He tried to cast a warning glance at Faithful, but the young man's focus was intently elsewhere. These scantily clad sisters had ensnared a new, more susceptible target for their wiles.

"The King, yes of course!" exclaimed the eldest. "Our father has been looking long and hard for a few strong backs to help reap our fields, you see. In service of the King, of course."

"Why would the King station you so far from the Narrow Road?" Faithful asked.

"It's not that far," the youngest answered. "Not really."

Christian could see it all unfolding now: the middle sister, who appeared only slightly older than her youngest sibling and was the most beautiful of the three, remained silent but kept Faithful's gaze locked on her eyes and playfully twisted a curl of dark brown hair with one finger. While she filled the eyes, her sisters filled the ears.

"We have no time for farming, I'm afraid," Christian said, making a deliberate turn toward the hill and placing a coaxing hand on his friend's arm.

But Faithful halted Christian's steps, and continued to stare at the middle sister, even as his words addressed his fellow pilgrim. "Surely there's no harm in staying for a few days to help this family. I for one would appreciate a few nights' sleep in a real bed."

Hearing these words made the women giggle in a manner that Christian found repulsive, but at least it broke the staring spell upon Faithful, who averted his eyes and began searching the stones at his feet. Christian used the new opportunity to press his case on his companion and did so almost at a whisper.

"I do not think it wise for us to dare venture even so far as a *step* from our Road without just cause."

The middle sister separated herself from the other two, and it was clear that she meant to address only Faithful.

"Our house isn't far," she said in her sweetest tone, "just on the other side of the hill. Help us for the afternoon and we'll give you a meal and a safe place to sleep. You can leave in the morning."

Faithful looked at Christian. "Serving those in need is not a just cause? Christian, they need our help."

Christian curled his top lip against his upper teeth and pressed them together in frustration against the crisis of conscience that Faithful had put him in. He was convinced that Faithful would, for the first time, turn aside and honor the request of these women above the exhortation of Interpreter and the Book he trusted to stay on the Narrow Road. How could he abandon his friend to possible danger? Christian relented with a shrug of his shoulders.

"Very well. *One* night."

"Fantastic!" Faithful slapped Christian on the shoulder good-naturedly, and then he turned to the sisters. "My ladies, we will help however we can."

"Wonderful!" the youngest sister piped out. She put her arm around one of Faithful's with the oldest taking his other, and they began to walk him along the path that circumvented the hill.

The remaining daughter matched herself with Christian, aroused by the challenge or maybe intending to get a jealous reaction from Faithful.

"You know, we're not merely looking for day laborers or hired hands," said the oldest sister. She leaned into Faithful's ear but still made sure Christian could hear. "We'd love to find husbands, as well."

The revelation made Faithful's cheeks flush, which he tried to hide by coyly looking to the ground. "You're all so lovely. I'm sure any one of you would make a fine bride."

The sister attached to Christian touched his arm for attention and fastened her eyes on his with charming tenderness. "And you, sir?"

Christian laughed. It seemed as though these women had never met a man before and were desperate for affection, or perhaps they were playing to every damsel-in-distress cliché they'd ever learned in an attempt to secure free labor.

"I am already married," Christian replied.

The women giggled and looked at each other in a way that Christian knew could not be good. If anything, he felt that his being married meant little more than an increase in the challenge, and a greater satisfaction in meeting it. He also began to wonder if their intentions might be even more sinister than he previously suspected.

"Where are you ladies from?" Faithful asked.

"We are originally from Hilekârlık, far to the south," replied the oldest sister. "Father moved us here when we were still children to be of better service to his masters."

The sisters guided the pilgrims away from the Road along the path around the hill and soon they could perceive a seemingly immobile old man sitting in an old, unhitched wagon. There was no cottage or abode of any kind in sight. The path descended out of sight into the steep hill they were meant to climb. However just before it left his view, Christian saw over the path a massive craggy rock jutting precariously from earthen walls rising up on either of its sides. It was very possible that the home and field belonging to the sisters and their father were located down that way, but Christian did not aspire at all to walk beneath such a dangerous outcrop.

"There's father up ahead now," Christian heard the youngest daughter say.

As they drew nearer to the cart, Christian kept an experienced eye on the old man, whose hunched back was toward them. There was something strange about the way the old fellow moved—*twitched* was a more accurate description. Distracted by his company, Faithful was not even looking at the cart and thus could not offer his fellow pilgrim any help in figuring out why this newest mystery only added to his rapidly growing unease.

The entourage was passing the fellow now, and Christian shifted his eyes to get the best look he could. It was all he needed: the shoulders of the elderly farmer were twitching because the hands and arms were shaking wildly, as if barely within the control of the frail human body, and his flesh was a sickly pale. Christian had seen such a creature before, outside the gates of Mansoul. "Old Adams", fellow Tracers had called them—decrepit men that were but shells of their former selves, made so either through torture or punishment. But this pitiful facade was what made the creatures so dangerous. They might appear as aged men but whatever inhabited them inside was far from human or harmless. He had never encountered an Old Adam away from Mansoul—he didn't realize they could exist away from such walls.

Christian stopped dead in his tracks. "What is this?" He yanked his arm from the deceiving young woman. Her surprised cry caused Faithful to look over his shoulder.

"Christian, don't be—" He reflexively snapped his eyes in the direction his companion was looking with such dread and betrayal.

With the reflexes and strength of a lion the Old Adam was upon Christian, swinging him around and driving the pilgrim back...back...back—their momentum increasing with each of the creature's steps—until they met the side of the rocky hill some forty paces away from the path with incredible force. Christian felt the air get forced from his lungs and his sight went momentarily dark from the impact. When his sight returned he almost wished he had been knocked unconscious because the Old Adam's face contorted horrifically and where there should have been eyes there were soulless pits.

The possessed being let out a shriek from a mouth that was unnaturally wide, and then leapt straight back from his prey. He cocked his head like a praying mantis, probably considering his next attack. But he didn't get the chance. Faithful shoved the creature forward into a face plant, stopped only to deliver a ringing kick to the side of his head, and then continued on to his friend. Christian offered a hand, which Faithful clasped strongly and yanked forward.

They were off, backtracking along the path in an all-out run to the fork where this whole nightmare had started. They couldn't escape the intense feeling that their adversary would not let them escape, but neither man dared to lose pace looking over his shoulder.

Within moments they saw their goal but entertained no notion of slowing their pace, not even for one last drink of the spring's sweet water. With Christian now just ahead of Faithful, they inclined their course up the hill figuring they would continue on a path that would intersect with the Road soon enough. Its steepness slowed them down quickly and they had not gone very far up the hill before they were gasping and nauseous from the labor of their climb.

A terrible cry from behind stole Christian's attention. He paused, snapping his head over his shoulder: nearby he saw the Old Adam had tripped Faithful onto his stomach and was dragging him down the hill by the legs while Faithful clawed for leverage among the rocky terrain. Without aid, Faithful's situation was hopeless.

Christian retreated to Faithful, grabbed his forearm, and pulled against the unnatural strength of the Old Adam. Faithful kicked as best he could to give Christian as much leverage as possible. The cooperation succeeded with Faithful getting in a parting kick that stunned the Old Adam just long enough for Faithful to scramble to his feet.

But the creature would not give up so easily. He grabbed a handful of Faithful's clothing, revealing a skeletally-thin hand. There was a roll of thunder and the being whipped around to face some unknown threat as if he were afraid of thunderstorms.

Though he briefly looked into the cloudless sky, Christian took no time to ponder where the thunder had come from before the pilgrims turned and fled uphill as far as their aching bodies would carry them, which ended up being less than halfway up the hill. Bent over double, with hands on knees, they sucked in air and were relieved to see that the Old Adam had not followed them. But neither had he left. Hissing with rage, the tormented creature cursed up a black storm of obscenities and blasphemies the likes of which Christian had never heard. Behind the creature, the three sisters were standing at the base of the hill gazing up at them all.

Suddenly the Old Adam's empty eye sockets widened and he pointed a bony finger straight at Faithful. "I know what is going on in that lustful mind of yours!" he wailed.

Christian glanced at Faithful, whose startled look confirmed that the charge was true.

With renewed strength, the Old Adam charged up the slope as if it were level ground. He was upon Faithful before they could flee, and beating him in a frenzy of blows with his grotesque hands. Christian's effort to pull the Old Adam from his helpless friend was met by a tremendous punch to the chest that sent Christian into a sliding roll back down the hill.

A wave of sliding dirt and rocks preceded Faithful, who soon tumbled past Christian having apparently been thrown into Christian's general direction by the Old Adam.

The Old Adam leaped down to them, clothes in flowing tatters, and pinned Faithful to the ground with a bony claw wrapped tightly around his neck.

"To the Lawgiver with you" he hissed, spittle and phlegm showering Faithful's face, "but not before I beat you within a very inch of your life!" He raised a skeletal fist to deliver the deciding blow.

"Yeshua...! Yeshua, oh my King...!" cried Faithful in a voice saturated with desperation. "...have mercy on us!"

Something like the crack of thunder erupted from the base of the hill, rolled up the slope and over the pilgrims, and froze the Old Adam in his place, though he still held Faithful tightly.

"I said: *release him.*"

This time Christian heard the voice through the thunder—in fact it *was* the thunder—as authoritative as a great commander and yet as soothing as the trickling of a stream. From his prone position, Christian could not see to whom the voice belonged, but he did see the creature give a start and turn his head down the hill. The Old Adam clearly saw someone with whom he could not contend and for the first time it was the monster's turn to be terrified. His body flinched as if the unseen and powerful force that already enveloped the whole area was growing (or moving) toward him. Then the Old Adam was gone in a bound, presumably back to his place on the other side of the hill. When Christian crawled over to confirm it, there was indeed no sign of the Old Adam or his daughters.

Instead, another form stood upon the Road, fully cloaked in a handsome robe, standing alone, and raising a beckoning hand.

"Come here," the Voice called.

The words were a gentle invitation, not an order; the voice sounded as if the person stood just beside Christian, and yet he was clearly many paces away at the foot of the hill.

A hand touched Christian's arm. He turned and saw Faithful standing there. He looked terrible, as if he had been dragged by a horse, and yet he stood there in his pain having also heard the voice. He nodded his head, indicating that he desired to go to the man—if indeed it was a man, for in fact it seemed more like a vision of a man— awaiting them. Christian looked again at the luminescent figure and swallowed. He could not refuse the invitation, or more accurately, Christian understood that he had the freedom to do so and yet he could not, just as a man dying of hunger had the full freedom to refuse a slice of bread but knew it would be a fatal mistake.

Christian put an arm around Faithful's waist so that his friend could lean on him as needed and together they descended the slope of parched grass and rocks.

The closer they got to the figure the harder it was for either of them to look directly at him. Less than ten paces away, Christian could see just below the hem of the robe that the person wore no footwear of any kind, but what he did see was a pair of pronounced scars atop each foot—evidence of puncture wounds. Christian's eyes moved up to the hands—strong, like a workman's hands—and they too had violent scars, a bit longer than those in the feet as they started at the wrist and disappeared beneath the sleeve of the robe. And what a magnificent robe! A thick line of dazzling snow-white sheepskin rode up the center from bottom to top where it was comfortably fastened at the chest and waist. As the sheepskin

עושי

reached the neck area the material widened to cover the whole of his broad shoulders and descended down his back. Separated by slim cords of metallic gold were vertical color bands of varying widths and textiles arrayed out from the sheepskin in a symmetrical pattern, with each color a broad span of cloth comprising stripped shades of evergreen, flame red, lily white, sunset gold, coal black, scarlet like that of blood, the purple of high royalty, lightning silver-white, rich jade, white-gold like snow reflecting winter's morning, and star-speckled cobalt like the hour before dawn.

Christian stopped and turned his head slightly toward Faithful, who paid Christian no attention with shifting eyes focused on the vision before them, and Christian concluded that Faithful had also noticed the scars and striking robe.

Christian turned back to the figure before them. Neither of them could see the face of the One Who had addressed them for it was hidden by the sheepskin hood and a pulsing glow of white light that seemed to radiate from beneath the covering.

From the corner of his vision, Christian saw Faithful fall to the ground. He thought that his dear friend had buckled from the beating he had received from the Old Adam, and when Christian shifted to check on Faithful's condition he quickly found that Faithful had fallen to his knees in reverence.

"My King!" cried Faithful. "I'm so...how can I...?"

Faithful's voice broke and in that moment Christian realized Who was standing there in such weighted silence, bearing the wounds of rejection and wrath that should have been theirs. Christian's knees bent and he joined his friend in the dirt, unable to look at the Face that would surely be revealed from this low place.

"I'm a rebel," Faithful finally continued. "I've served Apollyon all my life." Although Christian did not look, he could hear his friend struggle with the next words. "What must I do to be accepted into your Kingdom?"

Christian heard shuffling but kept his eyes forward, too nervous now to even look at the Man's feet.

Yeshua directed His first response to Faithful. "My son, why is your heart still troubled? You have placed your trust in Me and so your sins have been forgiven. Trust in El Shaddai. Trust also in Me. You will abide with Me in My Father's presence, forever. Now take up your cross each day and follow Me."

Faithful responded through sobs: "Yes, my Lord!"

Yeshua turned next to address Christian. "And you, Christian? Will you follow Me?"

Yeshua's words brought images to Christian's mind that he could not reflect on, for a discomforting quiet ensued and the pilgrim knew he must reply.

"Sir, my family..."

"Can a man plough the field while looking over his shoulder? Are you not ready to turn from your sins and trust in Me, Christian?" The inquiries were firm but not quite rebuking.

Christian's mind raced. He heard the questions and his fallen mind had a ready answer. How can you ask this? it was screaming. How can anyone understand who had no family? And have I not already turned from my sins in that I no longer serve Apollyon?

Christian knew that his service to Apollyon was not his only sin, and furthermore the King was not merely asking about his willingness to repent. Yeshua was telling him plainly: If you are not ready now, then when? If an exception is made now, how will you meet temptation in the future? His former mentor had told him to stay the course and walk the Narrow Road, for his steps would be the ones his family would follow. But if he turned back and survived long enough to meet his family at the elder's sanctuary, Christian would be assailed with doubts and wonder which new situation might cause him to again turn his steps away from the east. Moreover, he needed to be sure this time—sure that he was leading his family down the correct Road—but how could he be sure?

Christian didn't know what other choice he had, and so he decided to continue along this Narrow Road to Celestial City and take his first steps in faith.

"I will do what You say, my Lord."

"Do you have such little faith, Christian?" This time there was a distinct rebuke in Yeshua's voice and Christian felt sure that Yeshua must have known his innermost thoughts.

"Lord, please help my unbelief!" Christian pleaded, softly.

"Very well, Christian. Continue on your journey to Celestial City, where you may receive the reward of faith."

Christian bowed his head, unsure what would happen next, but his heart leapt. This was all a test: he simply needed to make it to Celestial City. If he could do this task then surely he would be granted his wish to help rescue his wife and children, maybe even as part of Yeshua's great army.

Yeshua moved toward them—to Faithful in particular. Christian turned his head just enough to be able to see what the Son of El Shaddai intended with his friend. The King knelt down, lifting Faithful's chin with one gentle hand.

"I Am the Resurrection and the Life. He who believes in Me will live even if he dies. Do you believe this, Faithful?"

Faithful nodded in affirmation and Christian was sure that his companion would never again need to ask if Yeshua had really conquered death.

Yeshua rose to His feet.

"Rise, my friends." When Christian and Faithful had obeyed, he continued. "By your endurance you will inherit what has already been prepared for each who places their trust in Me. The forgiveness of transgressions is won. Believe, and you are saved from the wrath to come."

He pointed to the Book, held close to Faithful's waist by his belt. "My words are with you. They are placed in your minds and written upon your hearts. My Spirit is with you. He will strengthen you in the trials to come, remind you of My words, and tell you what to say. But you will not see me again until you reach My City."

Then the vision of Yeshua was quickly overtaken by a brilliant light, forcing Christian to avert his gaze. As He was taken from their sight, Yeshua's voice imparted these final words: "Do not fear what you are about to endure. Be faithful unto death, and I will give you the Crown of Life."

Christian and Faithful stood alone on the Road at the foot of the hill. Several moments passed where neither said anything to the other. But after a while, Christian began to feel an increased anxiety about their lack of progress in climbing this great hill before dark.

Christian, followed in silence by Faithful, commenced the test by entering through a simple path marked by two flanking stone pillars that were shoulder-height. The Road itself was made up of sun-worn grass stubble growing up through well-trodden dirt and to the left a small brook from a gap in the hill babbled its way to the spring that had refreshed them earlier.

Faithful had taken the brunt of the attack from the Old Adam, but he was young enough to recover from his injuries more quickly than Christian could have. Christian wondered which of the two would be sorer in the morning, but he didn't like his chances.

The initial incline was not quite as steep as the side course they had taken to flee the Old Adam. The Narrow Road cut through a rough, shallow valley for a mile or so, after which the Road rose up onto flattened terrain comprised of parched dry-grass and patchy overgrowth of various types atop random stone formations. There was a short plateau and then up they climbed again for well over an hour, staying close to each other for aid as high rock outcroppings to their left often threatened to push them off the cliff to their right.

The pilgrims were provided a brief break from these dangers as they came upon several collected humps of hundreds of large boulders strewn about on all sides. When this was conquered, the Road leveled again and they soon came to a waist-high picket gate with a wood nestling both sides of the road on the far side. Just beyond the gate the Road inclined with small trees and fresh ground foliage shrouding the view any further than thirty paces ahead. When their surroundings finally opened up, the pilgrims thought they had trespassed into someone's garden: thin white birches, yellow common broom, patches of sky-blue irises, stick plants that appeared like flames, and shrubs of pinks and purples—snowbells, azaleas, rhododendrons—lined both sides of the footpath for miles. It was a dreamscape that cruelly tempted the exhausted pilgrims to rest, though they were still determined to make up for lost time and put as much distance as possible between themselves and the Old Adam.

Eventually, an arbor came into view on their right. They paused and noticed there were all manner of decorative Crosses upon it. When Faithful noted this, and that it was connected to the path, they decided it must have been placed there for weary pilgrims and it might be a good idea to finally take a brief rest.

*　*　*

Awake, Christian jumped up to his feet, new life coursing through his stiff legs, unsure of how long he'd been dozing in the peaceful arbor. Faithful had to follow, and on they went.

The Road through the gardens became a walkway through wonderful rolling terrain dotted with trees rustling with the late afternoon breezes. After nearly an hour they came upon a tree with a squat stump and at least a dozen large branches jutting out from the thick trunk and then turning into the air at great height. It appeared to Christian and Faithful like a large creature with many arms inviting weary travelers to camp beneath its protective canopy or nap upon the branches out of reach of any passing wild beasts. They paused to lean upon one of the branches and Faithful commented on the good terrain.

Christian knew that Faithful was subtly proposing that they rest here for the night. He looked to his right and found that he could view the far southern horizon with great clarity. The cliff-edge of the hill was nearby as well, and just below it the tree-topped peaks leading for miles.

Christian turned to his companion and shook his head—they had to keep pressing on to the hill's pinnacle. The more they moved, the more unlikely it would be for the demons to find them.

"I think we should cover as much ground as we can," he advised. Faithful sighed, and then shook his head in agreement.

Making as much haste as their bodies allowed, the pilgrims found themselves upon the great hill's summit just as the sun was touching the horizon behind them.

"We'd better hurry if we want to find a suitable place at the bottom to camp for the night," Christian said as he watched Faithful take a drink of water from his rations.

"I don't think I can move another step," his companion complained with a swallow of the water and a gasp.

"Shall I roll you down the hill?" Christian joked in an attempt to lift his friend's dwindling spirits.

Christian assessed the terrain and did not like what he saw, nor did he have any patience to rest. They were paying dearly now for the time lost contending with the three sisters and the Old Adam. It would have been far better to travail this terrain in better light. He strode over to a clearing at the edge of the rock face and peered over the edge, then enthusiastically motioned Faithful over.

The moment his friend was beside him he pointed down at what lay on the other side of the forested peaks to the east: a lush green valley, which by all appearances led into a wide meadow. Just then a breeze passed over them from the east, which carried the fragrance of that valley and field.

Faithful looked at Christian with exhilaration at the sight. "If that is what lies at the end of this difficult hill, I can wait to rest...if we hurry!"

The pilgrims quickly returned to the road and passed through a long tunnel of over-arching branches from scores of trees edging the Road, the leaves radiating in a dazzling sunset. With renewed vigor they continued down the eastern side of the hill, into the looming twilight of evening. But less than an hour later, the last of the amber sunlight barely painted the tips of the tallest standing stones and trees far above them. Dusk would be on them even faster with the ambient glow of the evening completely blocked by the hill.

"We'll never make it to the bottom before dark," Faithful observed with fret.

"True," replied Christian, "but fortunately we are moving downward and the slope is not too steep. Also the terrain is nothing like that coming up. It is flat and wide, with few places for animals to lurk or for us to stumble. And remember, this Road will guide us safely to our goal."

They were given another blessing: a half-moon that provided a wash of light to aid their navigation just in case anything should ambush them.

For nearly two hours they made good progress down the hillside. At a rocky alcove where the Road channeled between two rows of soaring pines, Christian stepped badly. One foot slipped, followed by the other. He stumbled and seemed to maintain his footing, but the earth gave way ever so slightly beneath his weight. His balance compromised, Christian threw his arms out to brace himself as he fell. He thought he heard Faithful call out in aid, but he was helpless to respond. A small rock slide carried him down the rocky hillside on his back, and away from the Road.

Christian prayed that they were near the foot of the hill when he landed with a *thud* and the contents of his travelling bag scattered in every direction over the ground. He was still for a moment, eyes closed as he tried to retain his composure, and then he realized how grateful he was that he no longer had a helmet packed away. The sound of Faithful's concerned voice was a welcome sound. Christian opened his eyes and turned himself over to a kneeling position. He looked down at bloodied hands and sighed.

Faithful finally arrived at his side and placed a sympathetic hand on Christian's shoulder.

"Are you alright?"

Christian held up his scraped hands, but otherwise bobbed his head in exasperation.

"I guess we'll camp here for the night," Christian said with a smile.

"I'm glad you didn't roll me down the hill after all," Faithful said. "That looked painful!"

Christian began to chuckle at the humiliating manner in which he had unceremoniously defeated the hill. Faithful joined in too, as he got out some strips of linen to bandage his friend's abraded skin. Christian surveyed their surroundings as Faithful began to gather the contents of Christian's kit.

They had come into a moderate valley. The hill descended gently, and from his vantage point it looked like the Narrow Road descended gently as well, which meant it would be easy to pick up again in the morning.

CHAPTER TWELVE

"This is...nice!"

Christian studied the scenery and found that Faithful had deeply understated his observation. It was an hour past sunrise and they could now properly examine the valley they had entered into after their misadventure the night before.

The pilgrims had come to a land that in the full light of morning was more emerald than any Christian had ever seen. Even before Mansoul had been over-run it was never so lush. Groupings of short maples and taller pines covered the rolling ground from the foot of the hill to the ridge behind them, their lush green foliage rustling with the crisp morning air. Where there were no trees or grass, lavender and red overgrowth occupied the space. It was a thoroughly idyllic image of a sort Christian thought only existed in fairy tales and legends.

Christian looked past the scene to the hill. He could see now that the curve to its eastern face was not more than a few hundred paces from them—which meant they had been very near to completing the journey when he slipped.

"We are still very close to the Road. Let's have our breakfast and then set out upon it immediately," Faithful said. Christian readily agreed, for he wanted to see if there was any more to this divine landscape.

They spent the morning of that day's journey entirely in the rolling emerald valley between two ridges with a wide river of crystal clear water, which tasted like honey, running along the north side of the road. The only change in their surroundings was the ridge on their right, which after several miles became a rounded peak twice as high as it was from its beginning.

As midday approached, the width of the valley constricted considerably and with it the channel of water so that it became more like a river. The ridge on their right receded from view behind a thick line of trees that were so close to Christian and Faithful that their branches often overhung the Road, and even at times reached over the riverbank.

The ridge to their left also reduced in height, and although it remained sloped, small white cliffs of flat-faced rock protruded from the earth at random intervals. The setting was so beautiful that the pilgrims were overwhelmed by the warmth of joy and a deep longing. They thought they must be near to the Celestial City. Only the urgency of their mission and fear for his family's safety kept Christian from truly enjoying what might otherwise have been a wonderful day.

By late afternoon, the pilgrims had emerged from the "long wood". The ridge on their right had completely vanished and was nowhere in view behind them. The ridge on the left was rising again; the river was becoming a stream, and now to the right was the widest rolling pasture either had ever seen. The land was robed in wildflowers of yellows, reds, purples, and whites. Further on they found some trees that provided fruit for their enjoyment and the further they walked the more of these trees they discovered. They ate their fill, refreshed themselves with the cool water, and stored as much fruit as their packs would hold.

With dusk approaching, the first clouds they had seen since climbing the hill stretched across the sky from ahead to the east. As they reached to the west the clouds burned like fire, changing to deep pinks and violets as the sun dipped beneath the horizon. To the south a small forest ran parallel to the Road, and a new pair of high ridges could be seen flanking the Road ahead. As Christian looked at the ridges, a frigid air passed that made him shudder.

"Perhaps we should make our encampment here for the night," suggested Faithful.

"I'd rather press on as long as the country is like this, but let's stop for food and a short rest."

Once a small fire was burning and the Pilgrims were wrapped tightly in their cloaks, Christian's chill retreated. Faithful delved into the Book for comfort, as usual, but didn't read far.

113

"I heard in one of the Palaces that the light of faith must shine through us to those we meet, that they may see our good works and glorify El Shaddai. I hope that my light may be seen by others…" Faithful's voice trailed off as he slipped deep into thought and began to read again.

Christian was not a man who typically shared his opinions or feelings without provocation. However, he couldn't help but think about how brightly Faithful's light shone to him each day, and he indeed saw Faithful's deeds and attributed them to his new trust in Yeshua. Faithful's light shone as brightly in this dark world as his father's light once had, albeit briefly.

Streamers of clouds, golden and grey, brought long shadows over the pilgrims, reminding them that dusk was upon them. They needed to press on.

Soon after starting they entered a narrow valley surrounded by stony ridges that crested far above them. A wind picked up, bringing with it a stale odor and humid atmosphere from further inside the valley. The light faded from the day long before the sun was fully set, so that it was nearly as black as night even though it was not yet twilight.

By the time the moon had risen, a fog had rolled down into the valley, casting their surroundings in ashen grey. Faithful noticed that the river, which by now was really just a thin stream, was abruptly ending. They filled their mouths and water skins with the honey-water one last time and continued onward.

Within a hundred paces, the gorge closed in upon them until the face of the ridge was vertical and close enough to touch on each side by simply spreading out one's arms. The Road constricted also so that the pilgrims were forced to walk single file—Faithful in front and Christian behind. This situation persisted and when they came to a pair of twisted, leafless trees flanking the Road, the pilgrims stopped.

"If it gets much darker…" Faithful began. "We have no torches."

Christian nodded and peered into the darkness ahead: gnarled and broken trees, similar to the pair that seemed to act as a kind of wooden threshold to their new test, lined the first several paces ahead. A warm breeze swept over them that carried with it the sulfurous tang of a smelting kiln.

"There seems to be a glow starting alongside the Road not too far beyond the trees ahead," Christian said after several moments of squinting past Faithful to get a better look inside. "We better press on since we do not know how long it will take to travail this place. We won't get much sleep here anyway."

With a sigh, Faithful agreed and resumed the journey. Immediately upon entering, Christian detected a difference in the atmosphere. All sound from the outside was swallowed up, creating a silence of the grave that Christian had never before experienced. The Road, which now seemed to descend, could only be navigated by carefully placing one foot in front of the other with cavernous pits opening often on either side. The pilgrims dared not reach out their hands lest they risk losing their balance and fall down some bottomless chasm...or worse, something grab at them from the pitch darkness.

It was impossible to determine time in this place. The only landmark that told the pilgrims they were progressing forward was the orange-red glow that was strongest on their left as it came ever nearer.

When they finally did meet this source of illumination, they were not sure they even welcomed it for it came from a source far below their sight. Indeed it only added to their unease. Strange shadows played against the rock face, including shadows that were not at all consistent with the flickering light source. In one case, Christian was sure that something had moved across the Road behind him—a thing that blocked out the light, except this should have been impossible unless the object could run across the chasm... Run? Christian thought. He kept this fear to himself.

"What was that?" Faithful whispered tensely.

"What...?" came Christian's earnest reply.

"Shhh!" Faithful seemed to be holding his breath. "That...!"

Christian strained his ears. "I don't hear—"

A hideous deep cackle intruded from a distance, presumably from the right, followed by a feminine shriek that raised the hair on Christian's arms. Next, a thick drawn-out moan widened the pilgrims' eyes. The source of the moan seemed to draw nearer to the pilgrims, causing them to draw their swords in unison.

"That was no animal," Faithful gulped. "What is this place?"

Christian had no answer.

"Is this what Mansoul is like?" Faithful inquired.

"No. There you can at least see what is moaning at you."

Another shadow moved nearby, and this one Christian and Faithful saw fully. Meanwhile, the clamor of wails, growls, and cackles grew in intensity and frequency. Christian and Faithful would have run if they could have, but they dared not trust the footing along the Road, even if it was straight. They would have to endure at a controlled pace, with swords held fast.

The smoldering incandescence brightened the terrain just enough to reveal, on the left, a deep crevasse between the Road and a precipitous mountainside. On the other side of the road lay an expansive exposed subterranean lake filled with putrid water. Christian stepped on something brittle that caved in beneath his boot and he heard a piece of the object fall into the chasm, but if it struck bottom the sound did not carry to Christian's ears.

The Road before them brightened in ghoulish hues of red and orange, but before they could get there the pilgrims had to traverse a Road that was just wide enough for them to place one foot in front of the other. They sheathed their swords, for they doubted they would be of much use against anything they met in this horrific valley and they needed to focus all of their attention on their footing.

Intermittently on the left, large gaps in the rock face revealed that on its far side flowed a river of molten rock—also the source of the glow that aided their progress. The setting flowed into Christian's mind, fed his dread, and reminded him of the terrible nightmare of Mount Apollyon that haunted his dreams. The veteran soldier shook his head as he tried to free his mind from any distraction that could lead to his doom, or Faithful's. It didn't work by his own power, but the rude incursion of black smoke and the most putrid reek that Christian had ever experienced certainly accomplished the task. He gagged and wretched at the new foulness.

The sheer rock face to the left suddenly ended, replaced by a wide crater filled nearly to the top with a hellish lake of lava. It bubbled and popped, sending drops of searing hot liquid-earth arching in their direction to splatter-*hiss* upon the edges of the foul lake.

Faithful gagged. "I don't know what smells worse, that wretched lake or whatever is coming from that!"

Both pilgrims wrapped their arms around their faces to block the rotting stench. A chant of doleful voices rose from the pit, and all around them were whispered blasphemies: temptations to doubt all the promises of reconciliation and immortality they had received from Yeshua, or that the words in the Book were lies as part of an elaborate deception conceived by men, accusations that El Shaddai was a fraud (after all, had they ever met someone who had actually seen Him?) and thus Yeshua had no authority to be King of even a blade of grass.

As the Road brought Christian and Faithful to the midway point beside the pit, sweet sirens mingled with the melancholy choir that grew louder and more distinct. It was all deeply exotic and spellbinding. Ahead Faithful was leaning forward to hear the choir better, heightening Christian's intrigue also.

Then a Voice came from his mind and reminded him of a quote from the Book that he heard his friend repeat just after an encounter with some of the nastier worldly folk they had met upon the Road: "Let them alone; they are blind guides of the blind. And if a blind man guides a blind man, both will fall into a pit."

Christian's head cleared and the mournful choir became mute. Just ahead Faithful was leaning forward above the precipice of the molten lake—leaning too far! Christian reached out to his younger companion, secured Faithful's torso in his arms, and fell back with all his weight against the Road. The collision with the hard surface jolted Faithful from the spell. He bounded to his feet with the reflexes of a fox and for several beats held his head in his hands.

"Keep your head, you fool!" Faithful whispered angrily to himself. "Christian, you saved my life."

"Let's keep moving," Christian replied.

"No," Faithful whispered. "No! The voice…he is pleading with me. He says he is my father."

"Your father is *not* in this place," Christian replied.

The siren-song rose again to ugly wails, pained and hateful cries against Christian and Faithful for not succumbing to their enchantment.

Christian threw his hands over his ears, but the terrible sounds seemed to pass right through his flesh.

"Quiet! QUIET!" he screamed hysterically. The pilgrims were barely able to ward off the cacophony when it was less intense, how could they hope to do so against the increased pitch?

Above him, Faithful offered a hand. Christian took it and was on his feet again.

Just as the men resumed their journey Christian perceived what appeared to be a pale phantom coming at them fast from the dark watery abyss on the opposite side of the path. What became of it Christian did not know, for Christian placed the hood of his crimson cloak over his head and focused on Faithful's voice, which now filled the space around them with the verses of a prayerful Psalm:

"The Lord is my shepherd, I shall not want. He makes me lie down in green pastures; He leads me beside quiet waters. He restores my soul; He guides me in the paths of righteousness for His Name's sake.

"Even though I walk through the valley of the shadow of death, I fear no evil, for You are with me; Your rod and Your staff, they comfort me...

"Surely goodness and lovingkindness will follow me all the days of my life, and I will dwell in the house of the Lord forever."

At the moment Christian's companion spoke the words of the Psalm, a new and comforting feeling overcame Christian. The light feeling was uplifting and warm, and so overwhelming that Christian believed he couldn't have imagined it. Christian took one peek at his surroundings and found that while the dangers were still very much present and alarming, he was less concerned about being overcome by the surrounding shadows and cries.

However, the more Christian stared the more the dangers threatened to overtake him. An army of terrible specters took form and shrieks chilled to the bone. Christian decided to turn his eyes once more to the Road, allowing his hood to block his periphery, and he focused on the words that Faithful was reading from the Book while Christian placed a hand on Faithful's shoulder to steady him and guide him from behind while he read aloud:

"I will say to the Lord, 'My refuge and my fortress, My God, in whom I trust!' For it is He who delivers you from the snare of the trapper and from the deadly pestilence. He will cover you with His pinions, and under His wings you may seek refuge; His faithfulness is a shield and bulwark.

"You will not be afraid of the terror by night, or of the arrow that flies by day; of the pestilence that stalks the darkness, or of the destruction that lays waste at noon...

"For He will give His angels charge concerning you, to guard you in all your ways. They will bear you up in their hands, that you do not strike your foot against a stone...

'"Because he has loved Me, therefore I will deliver him... he will call upon Me, and I will answer him; I will be with him in trouble; I will rescue him and honor him... and let him see My salvation.'"

Faithful paused and Christian was sure that something swept by his cloak so close that he could feel the garment give with the impact. He thought of the apparitions he had briefly caught glimpses of and his pulse quickened at the notion of enemies that could not be fought with a sword or fist. He wanted out of this place! Even the thought of being back in Destruction at the height of the wrath in his vision seemed almost more desirable than this place where both light and hope seemed to be on the very edge of extinction.

Christian turned his head as he walked onward and became aware of two things: the Road was inclining, and a great song was rising up around him sung by unknown voices:

A mighty fortress is El Shaddai,
A bulwark never failing;
Our helper he amid the cry
of mortal ills prevailing.
For still our Ancient Foe
does seek to work us woe;
His craft and power are great,
And armed with cruel hate,
On Earth is not his equal.

If we in our own strength confide,
Our striving would be losing,
Were not the right man on our side,
The man of God's own choosing.
Who asks who that may be?
Yeshua, it is He;
Lord Sabaoth, His Name,
From age to age the same,
And He must win the battle.

And though this world, with devils filled,
Should threaten to undo us,
We will not fear, for God has willed
His truth to triumph through us.
Prince Apollyon is grim,
We tremble not for him;
His rage we can endure,
For lo, his doom is sure;

One little word shall fell him.

That word above all earthly powers,
No thanks to them, abides;
The Spirit and the gifts are ours,
Thru Him who with us sides.
Let goods and kindred go,
This mortal life also;
God's truth abides still;
His kingdom is forever.

The hymn began anew and this time Faithful joined in with the singing voices insofar as he could remember the words. Even Christian found comfort in the words and hummed the melody to keep his mind off of his present darkness.

Suddenly, from all sides came a blast of wind—the sweet air of wildflowers, mountaintops, and pine trees.

"We're out," Faithful exclaimed. "Praise El Shaddai, we have made it safely through!"

The world was still dark beneath a clear canopy of glistening stars, but otherwise the Road ahead was inviting. The men continued to walk for some time before they looked back over their shoulders and found that the valley of death was long behind them and shrouded from their view by low clouds. They walked for another two miles until that terrible valley was completely out of view. By that point, they found themselves in a delicate wood whistling with the gentle breezes of night and washed in a moon they could not see.

"Do you think that was the valley of the shadow of death?" asked Faithful.

"It seemed more real than shadows," said Christian.

Each pilgrim selected a nearby tree and they sat their weary bodies down for a rest. They were asleep almost immediately and attended by celestial creatures they conjured up from the dramatic events they had just passed through.

CHAPTER THIRTEEN

Upon waking to a warm blue sky morning, Christian and Faithful felt quite invigorated considering all of the things they had encountered in the hellish gorge. An Evangelist Palace emerged not an hour from where they had spent the remaining night hours but, much to Faithful's surprise, Christian would still not enter.

"Christian," Faithful urged, "you have made your decision to embark upon this journey toward Celestial City in the service of Yeshua! Why do you still refuse the refreshment of these Palaces?"

"I don't deserve such refreshment while my family suffers for *my* mistakes. And how can I look upon these kind faces knowing that I have killed so many of their companions?" Faithful attempted a retort but Christian cut him off. "My friend, I respect your piety. These Palaces are for you."

Eventually, resigned to the fact that Christian wasn't yet ready to partake in the teaching and fellowship provided by the Palace, Faithful let the matter die.

The younger pilgrim turned into the Palace sanctuary to receive fully of its benefits of instruction from the Book and to partake in the Lord's Supper, and after being taught more of the victory of Yeshua over demons and death, Faithful returned with provisions for both pilgrims and the men ate breakfast together.

Refreshed and ready for the work before them, Christian and Faithful took leave from their hosts with thanks and set out upon the Narrow Road to see where it would lead them next.

Just after noon, the lush open terrain had shifted from gentle slow-rolling hills speckled by trees, golden flowers, and a thick line of distant woodland to one of high flanking hills—its gradual rolling slopes quilted by gardens and vineyards. The air was humid, but there was a regular twist of wind that kept the heat from being unbearable.

ON THE
NARROW ROAD

"Will this summer ever end?" Faithful asked as he wiped sweat from his forehead.

Christian's focus was on the horizon and what appeared to be a large city. "I think we have greater concerns than the seasons."

Faithful squinted to the east in the direction Christian was looking and found a city far in the distance, apparently just to the north of the Road ahead.

"Do you think the Road will go through it?"

Christian shrugged. "Only one way to find out." Then he indicated a line of trees that shaded parts of the Road on both sides. "At least we will have some relief from the hot sun."

The pilgrims resumed their journey and soon met the entrance to what appeared to be a well-tended garden of high cypress trees and tall hedges. The Road cut through its center, descending enough so that the horizon was blocked from their immediate view. There were intermittent breaks in the vegetation that revealed aisle spaces bordered by more hedges, some of which had openings that led even deeper into the garden.

This setting accompanied the pilgrims for two hours before it eventually led to an arbor that arched over the Road and Christian and Faithful continued on for hours more with no end in sight.

The pilgrim's felt uncomfortable pausing for even a moment, partly because they felt like they were trespassing and partly because the garden was lined with sculptures and fountains of classical design; sculptures that mostly depicted triumphant men of war, statesmen, and officials of law but in some cases, the further on they walked, the figures appeared to be pagan gods and goddesses—thus increasing their discomfort.

However, night was fast approaching and the pilgrims were running out of options.

"I don't think we have much choice but to make a place here for the night," observed Christian half-heartedly, pausing at a small alcove in the hedges where a marble statue stood before a stone bench.

Faithful was clearly not comfortable but seemed to understand the situation. "Well, the Road is clearly marked, and this bench is nearby."

"We will make no fire tonight," Christian stated to Faithful's agreement. They had little choice but to be alert, so they decided to sleep in shifts and to leave immediately at first light.

* * *

When the restless night had turned to morning twilight, Christian and Faithful continued on. The garden ended less than half an hour later, and the city they had seen from a distance the day before was now before them, bordering the Road to the north.

The pilgrims stopped, peered over the side of the Road, and saw below that the Road was set upon a high bridge that joined two steep hills of plain olive-colored short grass, with a small stream running between them at the very bottom.

Christian returned his eyes to the city: it was from an age long passed (or at least made to look that way) with stone streets that cut through row upon row of rectangular colonnaded buildings, ornately designed basilicas, and open-topped arenas—all constructed of marble, concrete mortar, and fine metals. Housing flats were clearly discernible by their ochre clay tiles. "I didn't expect to see cities of this size so far east," Faithful said softly. "Unless—"

"This is Vanity," Christian said, completing Faithful's thought. Both men grew uneasy.

"So this is Apollyon's easternmost capital. I'm surprised that the Road comes so near to a city rumored to be so...vile."

"Indeed," Christian said. "Let's move past Vanity with as much haste as we can muster."

Faithful nodded in agreement. "I suppose we were bound to meet his cities at some point." Faithful briefly went up on his toes to look over the side of the short plaster-and-stone wall that now lined the Road past the bridge.

The streets of Vanity were remarkably quiet, and it was several moments before Christian and Faithful came across any other living souls. When the short wall on the side of the road came to an end, the pilgrims passed a half-dozen soldiers who were alternating between tacking up their horses and warming themselves beside a large fire. Christian made eye contact with one of the soldiers and an uneasy feely came over him.

"I think we better get on—"

"Christian!" Faithful exclaimed, pointing to the symbol of Apollyon etched into Christian's leather breastplate, which was now burning a fiery red.

"Wha—?" Christian muttered before finally realizing that this symbol was no mere decoration, but must be the means by which a Tracer's demon overlords located their servants in the field. Christian's discovery came too late.

The situation was nearly as bad as Christian could fathom: Belial, followed by several mounted soldiers, was coming along the Road with the sound of galloping hooves. Christian grabbed his young friend by the shoulder and they took off across the field. It was hopeless of course, and they were quickly surrounded.

The two pilgrims unsheathed their swords to the moderate amusement of their would-be captors. This chuckling ceased when they saw that their demon captain was in no mood for such a confrontation. Belial, wielding a jagged spear, was out of breath and seething.

"Your flight is over," he wheezed.

Christian maintained his composure and flicked his gaze across the brightening horizon. "It's getting lighter. Long night...*Belial*?"

"Give me an excuse to slay you where you stand," the demon hissed.

That was interesting: an excuse? Christian maintained his posture and silence, but Faithful could not help acknowledge the statement. He leaned into Christian's ear and started to whisper—

"Silence!" Belial snarled. A swift motion of his spear had Faithful disarmed. Next, the spear point found Christian's neck. Christian gave no reaction except to drop his sword as well. The demon circled the two men with growing satisfaction. Then suddenly he was beside Faithful, pulling his head back cruelly by his hair before shoving him to the ground. "Do you know how it feels to die?"

"Care to tell us?" Christian was not trying to be unnecessarily antagonistic; he just didn't want to see his defenseless friend slaughtered before their situation had a chance to turn for the better.

Belial growled angrily, and then said, "Once Vanity's High Council has judged you—for all humans to see—I will torture you until you plead for death's release."

Christian was about to sneer, but the *crack* of Belial's spear staff across his ear brought darkness instead.

CHAPTER FOURTEEN

Christian was awakened by the loud squeaking of an opening iron prison door. Faithful tried to help him up, but two guards entered the chamber faster than Faithful could move and as a result what Faithful would have done kindly was instead accomplished with careless spite. Christian was shackled, but he pushed the guards off with his shoulders and emerged from the cell under his own strength as the world continued to swim from his knock to the head. An extra pair of guards flanked Faithful to ensure that no trouble would come from him as he, too, was escorted from the cell.

Several flights of stairs later, the group emerged from the prison onto a dusk-shadowed street that could fit about twenty men lined shoulder-to-shoulder. Each side was edged by a long cement structure. The nearest, the prison building, was three levels high of well-crafted classical architecture: the ground level was lined with columns atop a set of short stairs, which were broken up in places by statues set into the stone. Fire-bearers lit torches beside closed doors along an arched path on the other side of the columns. The two higher levels contained rows of windows, and the building was perfectly geometric down to the intricate designs along the sides of the door frames.

Less than a hundred paces away, the street met a large concentric plaza and at its center was a beautiful round marble structure as high as the colonnaded prison building and accented by designs of pure gold topped by a tower that climbed into the sky. Christian had heard of this building before: the Hall of the Vanity High Council.

The inside of the Hall was vast and shrouded in deep darkness except for an elegant fire pit at the Hall's center that quickly took over for the fading natural light that still managed its way through the single line of small windows just beneath the ceiling far above. The chamber echoed even the slightest whisper or ruffling of cloth.

The prisoners were made to stand before a raised black marble platform, behind which sat six elderly councilors adorned in layers of fine white tunics beneath heavy ashen robes.

Suddenly, the fire pit sprang to life as if an invisible shaft were feeding it fuel, and out of its flames rolled another steel breastplate that transformed with the aid of a fresh pair of human eyes, as Christian and Faithful had seen before, into the physical form of a demon. This time, the demon was Belial. The demon-lord did not remove his gaze from Christian and Faithful as he strode up the platform to take a place in the shadows between the two middle elders, and Christian felt intense disgust at the manner of Belial's arrival.

The council member to Belial's right picked up his gavel and slammed it down twice.

"You two are hereby charged with desertion, sedition, and murder," the voice rattled, cutting right to the chase.

Christian retorted, "Murder?"

"Silence!" the rickety voice quickly followed. He studied Christian for several beats. "Like your superior, here," he continued, motioning toward Belial, "you are residents of a great City of Lord Apollyon, are you not?"

The older pilgrim sighed. "Can we skip the formalities?"

"You are facing very serious charges," the judge scolded.

"This trial is a *farce*," said Christian with eyes on the fire portal, making sure to vent some of his disgust on that last word that echoed around the hall. The response yielded unhappy whispers amongst the six councilmen. "We shall receive no justice here."

"I see," the elder council member finally replied before shifting his attention to Faithful. "And you? Have you anything to say in your defense?"

Christian watched his companion think, but it appeared more like he was ordering words that he had already prepared for this moment. When he spoke, his words were directed to the inquisitor but his eyes often met Christian's.

"I was the first to attack our Captain, Belial." Belial growled in protest at the utterance of his name, but Faithful continued undisturbed. "What I did, I did not do lightly. I certainly never meant harm to my true friends."

THE COUNCIL OF

VANITY

Faithful then looked intently at all the elders sitting before him, and then at the guards he could see.

"I, like you, was born under the rule of King Apollyon. I did not choose this life for myself, but neither did I know of any other. Yet all my life I knew that there was something wrong. My conscience was screaming out against my actions. You must feel it, too."

Several of the old judges shifted in their seats, but there was hardly any other reaction to Faithful's remarks. The young man took a few steps forward, which caused several of the guards to grasp their sword hilts. Christian also stepped forward, ever so slightly, in case he needed to intervene.

"One day," Faithful continued, "a so-called enemy spoke the truth to me. An Evangelist gave his life to warn me as I warn you now: there is danger all around you."

The chamber came alive with whispers. The resonating effect of the hall made it seem as if there were hundreds watching the proceedings. The aged council members looked on with renewed interest at the entertaining spectacle before them.

"We have been lied to—all of us," Faithful added over whispered protests before continuing, "and we are not safe. Apollyon seeks to destroy every last human." Many whispers were now turned to denouncing outcries. "I have come to know the fury of the True King against the deceivers and the vile work of demonkind. Flee from the wrath to come!"

The council erupted in outrage.

"Silence!" screamed the only judge who had spoken to this point. "This is madness!" he added to his first order, along with repeated raps of his gavel.

"This is treason!" barked a hatchet-faced elder on the other side of Belial, his delivery of the words forcing him to his feet.

"We know the true king, and it isn't the One of whom he speaks!" bellowed another, plumper councilman.

Christian had more than his fill of the whole charade. He had to get back out into the street where there was at least the possibility of making a run for it and causing a chase through the many streets that made up the city. "Enough talk! Do what you've been ordered to do!"

The judge holding the gavel, who must have been the chief elder, raised a hand in protest to the groans of his colleagues. Christian stepped forward next to Faithful and eyed the closest sword he could find. Meanwhile the elder that had stood returned to his seat, and the council was silent.

"We must maintain the rules of this court," the senior judge pointed out, "regardless of any personal feelings we undoubtedly have on this matter. According to our laws, all citizens have the right to respond to their charges."

Christian sneered. "Apollyon cares nothing about human laws—just or unjust—nor do you."

The hatchet-faced councilman thrust out a finger. "More treason! Are these the best cases you can present for yourselves?"

"The truth is recorded in the Book of Yeshua's Word," added Faithful before any elder could protest, "by those who were the first followers of the True King, and also those who proclaimed His first coming for generations. The men who were the first Evangelists saw Him killed mercilessly, and afterward he was raised to life again until He was hidden from human eyes in this world. Don't you see the immeasurable worth of the King's death for us? His bodily resurrection seals the victory over Apollyon, his demon-brothers, and the curses they spread to us! Yeshua's Atonement is the greatest demonstration of love in history. Yeshua the King is the Son of El Shaddai, the Creator of us all. His Spirit is watching us now. The True King is returning—I have seen Him!"

"Silence." The word came out unnaturally through the chief judge's clenched teeth like an arrow from a bow.

Dark smoke began to pour from the fire pit and a smoky form oozed, almost snake-like, across the floor into the shadows near Belial and finally settled over the elder, who cocked his head as if to better hear whispered utterances. The chief councilman nodded once, and then turned his dead-eyed gaze to the prisoners.

"Very well," he said, and then he looked at each of his peers individually. Each in turn gave him a curt nod. Then he raised the gavel and *banged* it out three times. "We enlightened humans know the difference between ourselves and the dogs who call themselves Evangelists." He looked at Faithful—or *through* Faithful might be more accurate. "'Atonement'... ha! 'Resurrection...' Myths for fools and fantasies for children." The elder shifted his eyes away from Faithful. "Since neither of you have a *reasonable* defense for your crimes, you are both hereby sentenced—"

The chief judge paused and appeared to be having a conversation with himself. "Uh huh," he mumbled. "I see. Very well."

Suddenly he lashed out his finger and pointed it at Faithful: "By the declaration of just human wisdom *you* shall be an example to all who would stray from the true path. All humankind shall bear witness to your cleansing, by fire, to be carried out immediately." Then he turned to Christian who, hearing Faithful's sentence, had turned to stare with horror at the evil fire portal from which Belial had emerged: "And *you* shall be released back into the heroic service of our Lord Apollyon, after you watch your friend die. Guards!"

Four of the armed men split off into pairs, grabbed the prisoners, and moved them toward a side portal. Christian was mortified and trying to process the verdict, yet he found some small relief in the fact that his friend wouldn't burn in the fire portal of "justice"! It also did not escape Christian's notice that some of the guards were hesitant in their postures, while others were eager for the opportunity to release some of their pent up intolerance and desire for blood—specifically upon Faithful.

Christian realized that Apollyon was forcing him into the same defeated position he had been in when he last surrendered into the service of Apollyon after the Great Rebellion, so many years ago. Christian would not submit to Apollyon's rule again, and he could not bear to lose another friend in this manner.

"No! Take me, let him go!" Christian said, doing what he could to muscle his way toward his friend.

More guards flooded the hall from outside and pushed back against the leverage of Christian's strength and determination. He cast a look over to the councilmen, who sat and watched as if nothing of note was happening. Christian could also detect the echo of a hissing whisper even though none of their mouths were moving. Of course!

"Apollyon!" he yelled in rage. "I know you're here, you coward! You might as well kill me now because I'll never again murder for you and your filthy minions!"

Belial leaned to the hatchet-faced judge who belted out: "We will burn your family!"

Christian felt his stomach drop. "Are they here? Show them to me!"

No, he concluded. If his family were truly captured these people would have surely trotted them out to mock him and attempt to turn him against Faithful. "High Council of Vanity, you lie for your masters. And they lie to you. They need us. They can no longer hunt Evangelists without human assistance."

The retort had an unintended effect: the guards ceased restraining him as his words at the least sowed confusion and doubt among their ranks. He used the moment to press forward to Faithful. "Run! I will take your place!"

His exhortation was met with welling tears in Faithful's eyes and a look that said Christian still didn't understand.

"I'm sorry, my friend. I've been prepared for this." Faithful grasped Christian with shackled hands, pushing the Book into Christian's belt as the men gazed significantly into each other's eyes. "I wish I'd asked you more about my father, though I suppose I will meet him soon."

Before any other words could be shared, Christian was yanked away, painfully, by his chains. The guards had recovered. They beat Christian into submission as they dragged him behind Faithful, who followed willingly through the door to stairs leading down to the Hall's inner open-air courtyard. A few steps from the bottom, Christian was thrown to the ground, with bits of dirt and grass kicked into his face for good measure.

Through the dust, Christian's dark surroundings came into focus and he saw the waiting pyre in the center of the courtyard. Faithful was being led up the pile of wood toward a stake at its center. The guards tried to grab hold of Faithful, but Faithful brushed them off defiantly. He stepped up to the stake and bowed his head in prayer. Meanwhile an armed man approached with a torch.

Suddenly, from a stone archway opposite his position, Christian spotted a hooded and winged figure enter the courtyard and walk toward Faithful. The being cast a magnificent glow of white upon everything, and yet no one reacted to her presence. The being seemed to glance briefly at Christian as she walked lithely toward the pyre and then up the wood pile.

His eyes stinging with tears, Christian watched the torchman touch the kindling and flames. The fire—slowly at first—began to encircle the still-praying Faithful. When he had finished his prayer, Faithful turned and looked directly at the lightening-

FAITHFUL

UNTO DEATH

white being. A wide teary-eyed smile bloomed on his face. Then he looked at Christian sympathetically.

"I'm sorry," he said in a voice that was inaudible to Christian, though Christian could read Faithful's lips.

The words were like a punch in Christian's gut. "No!" Christian screamed.

Faces turned toward him, and several more lit torches were thrown onto the logs and kindling of the pyre as people shouted, overcome with bloodlust and fury. Faithful turned to face the glistening-robed figure as the flames gained momentum and rose like a wall to envelop him.

Christian tried to peer through the flames to see his companion or the being with him. But he caught only glimpses.

Suddenly, Faithful's voice tore through the veil of fire: "Where are you Belial? Where is the death you promised me? Where is your victory? Praise El Shaddai, Who gives us victory over death through His only Son, our Lord and King...!"

Christian touched his face to the ground, clutched at the dirt, and wept.

CHAPTER FIFTEEN

Christian sat on the floor of the cell that he and Faithful had occupied together just an hour before, where he had been dragged after his friend's martyrdom. A fresh round of sobs shook his wearied frame as he thought of how it should have been *him*, not Faithful, who should meet so cruel a death. He was responsible for Faithful. And what would become of Deedee?

When the sobs ceased, Christian folded his legs up and placed his head, throbbing from dehydration and the blows it had received, into his hands.

What now?

Christian had been dumped back into this prison to be tortured by guilt and memory, and when his captors believed the initial shock was gone they'd probably come to take him back into the service of Apollyon as a Tracer—or worse. It was more likely they would bring him to Mansoul to break his spirit fully, unless they were even more desperate for Tracers than he realized. Knowing the kind of heinous acts committed against the enemies of Apollyon, Christian concluded they would ultimately succeed in breaking his spirit. After all, they had ways to keep a man from dying if they wanted, and every man had a breaking point. But they would find their task more than a challenge. And maybe, just maybe, Yeshua would feel him worthy enough to be consoled by a Celestial being like the one that had come to Faithful.

Christian doubted he had proven himself to hope for such a graceful release. His faith was nothing like Faithful's had been. Even in death, or perhaps more so because of it, Faithful's light had burned so brightly that Christian could no longer deny the saving power of Yeshua's sacrifice. Christian himself had seen Yeshua alive. From this point on, Christian would no longer live for himself: he would live for Yeshua as Faithful had.

A new round of sobbing overtook Christian as he thought about how he would never be able to tell Faithful how much his life and sacrifice had meant to him...at least not in this world. It wouldn't matter for long, though, as Christian's own suffering was sure to follow soon enough.

Perhaps Yeshua thought it right to test him under true suffering, and how could he argue? His family was always foremost in his mind on this journey, which he knew was unacceptable to Yeshua. And yet, Faithful had gone to his fiery death with El Shaddai in his eyes and Yeshua on his lips. The words in the Book had seemingly assured his heart that his mother would join him in Celestial City somehow. Perhaps that had been his prayer. Christian knew how close they were; he knew how much Faithful would want her to be with him and to share the joy of the King's atonement with her. Somewhere during their travels he had been able to leave her decision to follow Yeshua entirely up to Yeshua Himself.

Could Christian do the same? He must fight! He must continue his journey to join Yeshua at Celestial City and plead with Him for the opportunity to return, with Yeshua's army, to retrieve his family. But ultimately, how much choice did he really have?

Christian felt the edges of the Book through his shirt. A shaft of moonlight hit the wall opposite him and he realized that there was enough light reflected back into the cell to read some of the Book.

He took the Book out from his belt and fanned its pages, landing at the back where a small pencil had been stuffed and he noticed writing in Faithful's own hand. Tears came to Christian's eyes as he read the following words:

I will finally face the consequences of my treason, if it can be called that. While I am hopeful that this Book has shown me the truth and given me the strength to meet death as a victory, I cannot escape the burdensome guilt I feel. I fear that I have failed my best friend with no way of making amends. If only he trusted in the King the way I have come to.

My last and only hope is that my death may be a sign to Christian, as the Evangelist's was to me. Perhaps one more victorious sacrifice can serve my friend and draw others to the King away from the wrath that is coming upon this world...a world so full of unbelief, pride, immorality, idolatry, fear, anger, hope-lessness, and destruction that it cannot receive the words of this Book.

Yet it is my steadfast hope that with this one life I have, if it be the will of El Shaddai, that I can be used by Yeshua to save even one other. Oh, what a blessed mercy that would be.

* * *

It was well into the night and the moon was far along its journey through the heavens, but it still cast enough light through the small barred portal of the lurching wagon cart for Christian to keep his bearings.

Gloom fought time and again to overwhelm him, but Christian resisted each attempt. Faithful's writing and the testimony he had given to the mock court had buried itself into his core. All told, Christian had been given nearly an hour in the cell to read the Book on his own for the first time since his youth, and oh what comforting words were written there! The unjust death of Faithful had imitated that of the far cruder injustice suffered by the King he and his friend had promised to follow (even if his initial agreement had been less than fully trusting). Pondering the fiery scene of Faithful's temporal demise kindled a flame that grew in his chest each time he reflected upon it.

If he ever survived his captivity, Christian would use the remaining empty pages of the Book to tell Faithful's story so that whoever should read the Book after him would hear of Faithful's obedience to the words therein.

Christian pounded on the side of the wagon.

"What do you want?" came the irritated voice of one of the unseen drivers.

"Where are you taking me?"

"Would you rather go back?"

Christian looked down at his shackles and considered the soreness that seeped to the bones of his ankles and—*BANG!*

The wagon careened violently, pitching Christian sideways, but it managed to stay on its wheels as filthy curses rained down from the two drivers.

BANG!!

This time the box-cart tipped over on its side. Christian felt the horses break free and rear as they charged away. This was followed by a screech—cut-off before it could finish communicating its horror—and then another short squeal that ended in a sickening grunt. Christian was all too familiar with the sounds that escaped the mouths of men as they were viciously slain.

He tried to shake off the effects of landing awkwardly on his neck when the wagon had tipped and thrown him against its wooded wall. The shackles made his attempts more challenging, but he knew that whatever had just killed the two drivers was likely coming through the door for him, next.

"You didn't think you were going to get away that easily, did you?" Christian turned to the door of the cart, at its rear, to find Belial's head peering at him through the bars of the wagon door and confirming that Christian was the primary target of this attack. Within moments the door was ripped from its hinges and Christian was dragged, by two demons via his bindings, through a wood thick with cypress and illumined by very little of the moon's light.

"Halt!"

The demons stopped and Belial came into Christian's view.

"Did you think I would forget *this*?"

The dark creature grabbed the Book from the place where Christian had tucked it away, giving rise to a rage more intense than Christian could have anticipated. Belial would not take that Book! In an instant the pilgrim felt its leather cover slap loudly against his cheek, the blow severe enough to send him to the ground without any way for him to break his fall.

"Unshackle the beast," Belial wheezed. "I want him to squirm."

The demons complied, and the moment he was free Christian was preparing to lay a fist against the head of the demon-lord.

However, before he was even on his feet, Belial had one of his taloned hands wrapped around Christian's wrist. He squeezed, forcing the prisoner's hand closed, and then Belial forced the blade of his spear under Christian's fingers against the flesh of his palm. He paused to look at his helpless captive for a moment, and then punctured a deep wound into Christian's hand, with purpose, before throwing Christian back to the ground to writhe in agony.

"I can make you suffer like your King," he spat, "if you wish."

An amusing thought passed through Christian's mind that he gave voice to immediately.

"Can it be? Am I not the only one who dares defy the will of your prince Apollyon? You would kill the most famous Tracer Apollyon has? The hero of the Great Rebellion? I didn't think you had it in you," he said with feigned admiration before laughing, though it was difficult and not welcome to the party that up until now was enjoying their sport.

One of the demons, which Christian recognized as his former bird-like "companion", hoisted him up roughly so that he was just barely standing on his toes. On his right was Belial, and beneath Belial's belt was the Book.

"You don't get it, do you?" Christian continued to antagonize. "The reason Apollyon is leaving his mountain to replenish his ranks?" Christian expected a backhand, but none came. Belial was curious enough for the time-being to listen. "In the end, Apollyon needs *me* more than he needs *you*. Without Tracers like me, none of you would last long upon the earth. We humans can smell your demon stench a mile away, and feel your icy presence. We can evade you, *and we can send you back to the fire.*"

The demon holding Christian looked at Belial for a reaction, unwittingly relaxing his grip just enough for Christian to find traction. Christian pushed forward on the balls of his feet and sent himself and the bird-demon tumbling to the ground. He bounced over the foe, and in the pale light Christian saw the hilt of a sheathed sword within reach against the demon's side. With the reflexes of a seasoned warrior, the weapon was in Christian's hand and quickly found its mark against the eye sockets of Belial's other hench-demon—the bear-like creature—who clumsily approached to subdue him. From a sitting position, Christian continued through the stroke in a circular motion, slowed slightly before completing the ring, and then thrust the blade down into the chest and Apollyon crest of the bird-demon who was still attempting to recover from Christian's first blow. Stabbing through the bird's eyes, the demon's shadowy liquid-smoke equivalent of blood dissipated quickly.

142

Christian could hear Belial tighten his grip on the pole of his spear as Christian stood to meet his foe, but the pilgrim couldn't grip his weapon as tightly because the blood from his hand wound slickened the handle of his blade. The pain that came with clasping the blade was also intense. Give me the strength to endure this, he prayed silently. The thought hadn't exactly been a prayer as Christian understood them, but the image of Yeshua's pierced hands, and everything else He must have suffered, flashed through his mind. Certainly One such as the King had great strength for Him to bear the task that needed to be done, and could therefore aid a follower about to face a dark enemy they both shared.

In the end, this was exactly the moment that Christian had been hoping for since his capture—he now had a chance to escape and the famous demon-slayer of the Great Rebellion couldn't help but smile as he faced Belial, intent to retrieve his Book.

"You have something that belongs to me. I want it back."

Belial cast the briefest glance at the Book in his belt before throwing his spear, which Christian dodged by only the thinnest of hairs. He nearly missed blocking the taloned strike that followed, and the next. Christian knew he would lose this fight quickly if he didn't create a little distance, so he threw himself on his back, which forced Belial into a headlong tumble propelled by his own momentum.

Belial didn't fall, which would have been ideal, but his tumble still gave Christian a few much-needed seconds while the villain caught himself.

Belial leapt the distance back to Christian in one bound and resumed his attack, grunts accompanying each swipe. His short talons were as strong as steel and effectively acted as ten dagger points stabbing and slicing in a flurry. Christian had often known demons to fight sword-on-talon when they had no other choice, but Belial's lack of concern for retrieving his spear was a true testament to his fury and strength. By the reactions of his enemy, it seemed that his blade contacting the demon's fingers was not unlike a piece of wood rapping against bone, and yet the demon continued.

Belial was skilled enough to mix in a series of well-placed jabs to Christian's ribs and head, and although these almost always landed, the pilgrim felt that these blows were better to absorb than one of the demon's black talon-tips. Still, there was no way Christian could keep up this kind of defense. With each body blow and knock to the head, he lost a bit more air and responsiveness.

Christian was aware of a tree just past his shoulder. He pressed his back against it just as an open-clawed hand descended on him. He ducked and buried a shoulder into Belial's abdomen. The move ended with Christian landing face first in the dirt and the demon fuming loudly somewhere nearby. Christian quickly concluded that Belial was likely reaching the end of his patience for a fight he expected to have been already completed.

Christian scrambled to his feet and found Belial finally retrieving his spear. The demon turned and took several large breaths. He wasn't injured, but he was laboring: the demon *needed* to end this fight, now.

Belial broke into a charge, which Christian parried. But he was caught by the staff across the back of his head when the monster stopped his run almost immediately and then executed a swift backswing with the end of his spearhead.

Christian yelped but spun to face his opponent anyway, with stars in his eyes and his head throbbing with his racing heartbeat as he set himself for Belial's next attack. They locked weapons—staff to steel blade—and the demon-lord pressed all his weight upon Christian, who immediately released the pressure by lowering his sword. The momentum carried him down to his backside again while Belial's torso stretched out exposed above him. Christian made an awkward upward thrust that sank the sword well enough into the villain's chest and through the Apollyon crest.

Christian stood, gasping, and looked down at his writhing enemy. "Think Apollyon will want you back now?"

Stabbing through Belial's human eyes, it was satisfying to see dread Belial's hideous face as his body smoked and crumpled like wet paper. He looked down at his hand, which would need tending somehow. He looked at his shirt and was about to tear a strip when he caught the faint aroma of a wood fire. The pilgrim looked about and saw Belial's spear lying in some sparse grass and curling and blackening the grass that came into contact with the spearhead.

Christian approached the weapon and touched the spearhead gingerly, confirming that it was as hot as a poker left in a hearth. Taking in a deep breath, he picked up the spear by the staff and without hesitation pressed it against his wound. He emitted no scream—he could not risk it for Vanity was still close and he did not know who else might be in these woods. Instead, Christian channeled all his fury and frustration

144

over the last days' events through his body to overtake the searing pain. When he was satisfied that the gash had been properly cauterized, he thrust the spear far from where he stood.

Finally, Christian retrieved the Book with a satisfied smirk from the smoldering armor of the demon-lord. In a moment of pure understanding, he placed the Book against the Crest of Apollyon still on his leather chest guard. A red glow turned to black smoke flowing around the Book. When he pulled it back, the Crest remained as an ashen design, and Christian believed that Apollyon no longer held any sway over him. Then the pilgrim pulled the cloak that his old friend had given him around his body and hobbled toward the horizon only just brightening with the coming dawn.

Christian had nothing to offer Yeshua now. But at least he would ensure that Faithful's story would be read by any who would possess the copy of the Book he now clutched with frustration and pain.

CHAPTER SIXTEEN

"I imagine you didn't make it far after fighting one of the demon lords," said John.

"I made it far enough," Christian replied. "I found a place to write of our journey and tell of my friend's heroic deeds. After that, I'm afraid it wasn't difficult for the Ogre to find a man screaming half out of his mind with exhaustion and grief. Seeing Faithful die like that...it just made my waking nightmares all the more vivid."

John put down the Book, wiping the remainder of the moisture from his eyes. "Your friend was courageous."

Christian resumed his search of the stone prison, just in case the tightness in his throat became a wellspring of grief again. "Yes he was, and firm in his belief. But he got his wish: he led me to Yeshua."

"Aye," John nodded, "and me as well."

Christian's throat swelled and his eyes filled with tears.

John's eyes narrowed, as if he was trying to perceive something from a great distance. Then he closed his eyes, and there was only the sound of slow dripping and Christian moving along the cave wall. Whatever the thin man was trying to do, it was not working and ended in a silent shudder of anguish.

"I can't remember her," he cried out. "My wife...I can't remember what she looks like."

Christian halted his search. "You have a wife?"

"*Had* a wife," John corrected. "I've been gone so long she must have moved on by now. Our world is a cruel place, even crueler for a widow. I *hope* she has moved on."

"I'm sorry." Christian bowed his head a moment, realizing that this man needed a friend more than a rescue at the moment. He moved to where John was leaning against the wall and sat down across from him. "Do you have any children?"

The scraggily-haired head and face moved back and forth. "Children? No. I would have very much liked to though. Instead I ended up here, in this stinking cave as a prisoner to this stinking Ogre!"

Christian winced against the years of pent up frustration and sorrow that bellowed from John's mouth. But here was his opportunity.

"I have a wife and children, and they need me. I must finish my journey to Celestial City. I can't stay here, John. Do you understand?"

John shook his head wearily. "I'm telling you, there is no way to escape. Despair is too strong!"

"But there are two of us and only one of him. I've fought monsters before, John. If we just work together, we can defeat this foe." Christian returned to his feet and walked to a section of wall just to the side of his desolate friend. With a great tug he removed a large stone. Debris fell from the ceiling and Christian nearly panicked, thinking that the ceiling was about to come down upon both of them. But the falling sand ceased like the last grains in an hour glass, and Christian decided that the cave would indeed hold. "I'll distract the Ogre while you escape through the door. When I follow, lock the door behind me and we'll trap him inside." Christian held out his arm toward his cellmate. "Are you with me?"

John stared at the arm, motionless, before finally grabbing on and smiling. "You're going to get us killed. But what do I care, I'm out of reading material."

Christian nodded and looked at the cell door, secretly hoping that it would be strong enough to contain a raging Ogre. "Okay. First we will need to get Despair's attention, which should be easy enough." He looked at John, who nodded.

Christian moved to the door, paused and looked back at his cellmate, and then started pounding on the door and shouting nonsense. John added his own brand of 'woops', 'hoys', and shouts. When this seemingly had no effect, John tossed the tin water cup to Christian while John retrieved the tray, and these were added to the clamor.

Finally, they felt the ground tremor with the footsteps of the Ogre—it had to be. They stopped their yelling and banging. Christian pointed to John and then to a spot that would place him behind the door when it opened. Then he moved to the opposite side of the door, picking up the large stone he'd dislodged from the wall.

The door flew open, with Despair's massive frame filling the threshold.

"What's all this racket?" he bellowed.

As Despair entered the cell to investigate, Christian took a running leap that ended with him shattering the rock over Despair's head with seemingly little effect.

"NOW!" he shouted, giving John the signal.

Despair turned to John, who stood frozen in place. The Ogre moved toward John, his hand raised to strike. Christian looked at the remaining chunk of wall rock in his palm—it wasn't large but hopefully he could make up for it with the rush flowing through his veins. With deadly purpose he strode up behind their enemy and connected the rock against the Ogre's head with enough might to break a warrior's skull. The giant howled and turned in furious pain to Christian with a strike from a calloused hand that flattened the pilgrim against the opposite cell wall.

Christian did his best to shake the stars from his eyes as he staggered to his feet. Giant Despair shook the small cell with a heavy grunt, no longer considering John an immediate threat.

"I'll make you wish you'd kilt yerselves when I gave ye the chance."

He lunged at Christian, who was trapped against the wall, his body not up to this challenge after all the abuse it had endured over the last several days. He called out, "Yeshua, save your new believers."

Suddenly, a Celestial Being in full-winged glory filled Christian's eyes and shoved him out of the way of the charging Ogre. Despair passed right through the angelic being, crashing with all his weight into the cell's stone face. The being was nowhere to be found, but there was no time to assess. Despair's collision with the wall had started a growing cascade of rock and dirt that promised not to end well for anyone trapped beneath it.

As the world of the prison came down around him, Christian darted through the chunks of earth and joined John in the hall.

Suddenly, John leapt back into the collapsing cell, risking life and limb to retrieve the Book, only returning to the hall at the last possible instant.

Both men took several gulps of air and quickly realized that it was not just their former prison that was sinking in upon them, but the whole of...well, wherever they had been kept (it could be the whole fortress for all Christian knew)! Both men sprang to their feet and flew toward daylight at the end of the long corridor. Then as if being coughed out by a great creature, they burst into the morning daylight. A dust cloud rolled after them, along with reverberations that confirmed the ruin of the place of their captivity. They could not be certain of the demise of Despair, and so the men made haste into a bordering meadow toward a low-lying stone wall a couple hundred paces ahead.

The pair had not gotten halfway to the wall when Christian heard a *thump* upon the ground behind him. He turned quickly to find John face down in the tall grass and blossoming flowers, sobbing. He gave the older man some minutes to let his emotion flow.

When it sounded as if John had regained his composure, Christian extended his hand and said, "Come, friend. We can rest a moment at that wall ahead."

John wiped his face and then took Christian's hand. "Thank you... Thank you."

When they arrived at the wall, which was not as low as Christian had first thought but low enough to peer over without difficulty, Christian's heart leapt at the sight: the Narrow Road, paved with meticulously cut stone! Edging its other side was a stream. He looked up and down the wall for a way through, and found a stile not far from where they stood, flanked by vines and a few small trees turning from green to yellow. He looked back to John with a smile.

"Is this your Narrow Road?" John asked.

"It is."

"Well then, you'll be needing this," said the man with the scraggily beard, whose gaunt arm was extended to Christian with the Book in his thin fingers.

"I suppose we will, but why don't you hang on to it?" Christian paused hoping John had caught his meaning. But John's eyes reflected a soul and mind too overwhelmed with his regained freedom. "Come with me."

149

John's knees gave, his eyes reddening with new sentiment. "I thought I would die in there," his voice wavered.

"John, come with me," Christian pleaded.

John looked at the book, took a breath, and gazed at Christian with a set face.

"To the end," he said.

Christian pulled his new pilgrim-friend up and the men walked along the wall to the stile. Nearby they saw a small stone pillar lying alongside the fence. It was square and no longer than Christian's leg from hip to knee. John bent down, turned it over, and brushed off its face—revealing engraved writing:

Over this Stile is the way to Doubting Castle, which is kept by Giant Despair who despises the King of the Celestial City and seeks to destroy His holy pilgrims. Beware.

John looked at Christian, who immediately examined the area around the stile and found an inset opening on top about the size of the pillar's base. "It goes here, I think."

"We better place it back, lest another pilgrim wander into this meadow and become captured in that dark place as we were…if it will ever again be a threat."

"Better safe than sorry." Christian took stock of the pillar's weight. "We should be able to lift this together."

John grabbed one end, Christian the other and they set the post back to where it could once again warn pilgrims to keep on their course. Then, taking a drink from the stream on the opposite side of the Road, the two pilgrims staggered onward upon the Narrow Road toward Celestial City.

CHAPTER SEVENTEEN

"There! We must stop," said John in a raspy voice. It was long past dark, which made it easy for him to spot the torchlight in the distance.

"Only if it's on the Road," Christian replied, his legs feeling like water. Both men, clasping each other around the waist for support, were bent over from weariness. But this new hope renewed their vigor and they quickened their pace.

After several minutes, with the torch-lit window in view just off the Road and the overhanging trees receded, the pilgrims were awestruck: the window was not part of some meek abode but a great manor—and the Narrow Road led directly to its front gate!

With weary legs and this stunning sight in his eyes, Christian suddenly stumbled to the ground, landing hard with a grunt. John knelt to help his friend up just as two massive lions leapt toward them, snarling and biting viciously and shattering the serenity of the night.

John shouted in fear with each snap of the powerful, tooth-lined jaws as Christian used what strength he had to push himself backward. The slowness of his retreat revealed an interesting detail: for all their threat, the lions seemed unable to reach the Road. Christian halted his retreat, summoned his courage, and stood up to test his theory with his recently strengthened faith. With eyes straight ahead, locked on the door to the manor, Christian placed one foot in front of the other. As expected, the lions bounded at him again, roaring, snapping, and swiping.

But they could not touch him. The lions were chained and, no matter how hard they tried, the animals were unable to reach the Road. Christian walked on as John looked on from behind, and when Christian reached the gate he collapsed to the ground in a heap.

* * *

Christian awoke to the faint sound of female voices singing delightfully to an accompanying fiddle from a direction he could not determine. Morning sunlight poured into the lavishly furnished single-occupant bedroom where a fire burned low in a nearby hearth. His wounds were freshly tended and the hand which had suffered so much ill from his battle with Belial was skillfully bandaged. In fact his whole body had been cleaned.

Christian surveyed the modest-sized room: the walls were a soft shade of yellow with white plaster designs and borders that swooped and turned like grape vines. Everywhere was the faint scent of fresh flowers, and laid out for him on a chair beside his ornate bed were his own well-worn but now-clean traveling boots and new clothes, at the center of which sat his tattered Book. Aside from another chair on the opposite side of the bed (which appeared to have been used recently judging by the white sheet that lay there) and a large multi-paned rectangular window, there was nothing else remarkable about the space.

Christian sat up, placed the Book on the bed's thick blanket, and dressed. Then he grabbed the worn Book, opened the door, and proceeded warily down a long corridor lined with windows just like those in his guest room. The direction Christian walked also carried him closer to the source of the music, which continued without interruption.

When the hallway ended, Christian found himself looking into a spacious dining room lit by a wall-length series of latticed casements. A great inset fire crackled against the far side of the wall. In front of the fireplace sat a large bull of a man with a friendly face hidden behind a bushy, wild beard in a silver raiment. He merrily played his fiddle while a group of four beautiful women, also arraigned in silver cloaks draped over colorful dresses, sang in accompaniment.

At a long table in front of a pile of half-devoured food sat another, a thin man of middle age. The man was clean-shaven and dressed in a simple tunic similar in pattern to those worn by the fiddler and women. He smiled as he watched the performance— and it was that lopsided smile that revealed to Christian the identity of the man he was looking at was...one he had just come to know as friend and fellow pilgrim on

152

the Road: John. Christian remained in his place, not wanting to interrupt the beautiful music that warmed his soul.

When the song ended, the fiddle player smiled at the newly-arrived guest with a gleaming set of teeth. "Ah! Pilgrim, you must be starvin'! I'll go fetch yer breakfast."

The announcement turned John's attention toward his companion. "Christian, there you are! I've made friends!"

Before Christian could move, the young women swarmed him and guided him to a seat at the same table where John sat.

"Well now, you look very well rested," said one. "Much better than when we found you, I should say. My name is Prudence—" and then she pointed to each of her fellow ladies "—and that is Charity, and the one next to her is her sister, Piety. Just behind them is Discretion, and the gentleman who went to prepare your meal is Watchful—he's the porter.

Christian tried to keep up with the names as they were connected to the faces. But something Prudence had revealed needed clarification.

"Found me?"

"Yes," Charity confirmed, "passed out at our gate...looking a little worse for the wear. And that one...!" She indicated John but was unable to further explain the state in which she had found his friend because her sister now chimed in.

"We often give aid to pilgrims in need of help and rest," said Piety. And then she added. "You must have been very brave to face the lions! They are there as a trial of faith and must be passed in whatever state the test finds you."

"We know how difficult the journey is," continued Discretion. "You see, the King—"

"The rightful King that is," Piety clarified quickly.

"—instituted His beautiful Palaces as places of rest and fellowship for weary pilgrims along the Road to Celestial City. This Palace is the only one through which the Road passes directly. And those that bypass this haven on account of the lions are surely the worse for it on account of the trials yet to come. Even those with little faith will press on past the lions with success, seeing not the trouble but only the refuge to which the Road leads."

"Are we far now, from Celestial City?"

154

"Not far," answered Prudence, "but the Road ahead is still difficult. And there is a greater danger."

The women grew silent and began to look solemn. Meanwhile, the porter returned with a large food tray and a big smile. He perceived the silence and searched every face in the room, his smile fading to a look of confusion with each glance. He placed the heaping platter of bread and fruit in front of Christian.

"Did I miss somethin'?"

The women lowered their eyes, embarrassed. Charity moved from her place to pour Christian a drink of water until the cup was overflowing. When she had finished, the pilgrim nodded and said, "Thank you. Please, tell me what danger you speak of."

The four maidens looked at Watchful, and so Christian finally did as well.

"Ah, that already," the porter said with a bit of a sigh. "I'd hoped to wait until after breakfast before we discussed *that*." Watchful inhaled deeply and then let it out with a big puff as he looked intently at his guest. "Well, you see, word is out that The Beast is on the prowl, killin' whatever and whoever he sees. Something is very weird indeed when Apollyon lowers himself to murderin' for his own necessities."

Christian took a drink and grabbed some grapes from a cluster. "Apollyon is indeed walking the earth to replenish his demon ranks. I saw him with my own eyes and believe that either this war is not going well for him, and his human servants are more difficult to come by, or worse, he is filling the earth with demonkind in greater numbers than I have witnessed in a long time. If the latter is correct, it can mean only one thing—"

"War is upon us," Watchful interjected and Christian nodded in agreement.

"We *have* been receiving pilgrims and Evangelists with much greater frequency," Discretion added thoughtfully. "Could it be that the King is also using His Spirit to call His people to repentance?"

Christian thought about Discretion's question and was intrigued by the thought of Yeshua using His Spirit in love to call His beloved children to a renewed relationship with the Father. He considered everything he knew about Apollyon and the present state of the world, as he understood it, and noted the vast difference between Apollyon's recruiting tactics—fear, slavery, and murder—and Yeshua's. Christian was now ashamed that he had ever considered Apollyon's rule to be preferable to

155

Yeshua's. He would no longer rationalize his wrongdoing as an attempt to make the best of a bad situation. He had chosen wrongly, plain and simple. All he could do now was repent and faithfully serve his new and True King.

Christian had recently learned from the Book that Yeshua had already defeated demonkind with His death and resurrection. Apollyon and the other fallen princes, flesh walkers, were not desperate but wanton evil desiring to drag as many of those made in El Shaddai's image as they could down with them into eternal damnation. The judgment upon their rebellion was final, so what would it benefit them to cease their sedition?

"Apollyon will never stop trying to corrupt the very souls that the Son has sacrificed Himself to save," said Christian, remembering the Great Rebellion.

Demonkind would never give up, and woe to those who could not see the danger. Any further speculation on Christian's part seemed as though it would serve no purpose, though Christian wondered if he had come closer than ever before to discovering Apollyon's true motives.

"Tracers with my experience and skill are highly valued," said Christian, "not just for what we can do in the fight against Yeshua but what we represent to our communities."

Common folk bowing a knee to the King was bad, but an elite, educated Tracer with knowledge of demonkind's plans and movements becoming a follower of Yeshua could not be treated lightly under any circumstance.

"Apollyon needs to make an example of me...as a warning to other Tracers," said Christian, putting the pieces together.

The demon-prince Apollyon didn't sneak about like his brethren. He walked the world with a haughty step, showing all his supreme confidence in his own power and daring any provocation he expected would never come. That must be at least one reason Apollyon had come to Christian's trial at Vanity, to let it be known that he wanted a challenge.

"Apollyon was at my trial in Vanity to see to it that I was punished publicly. And to use my family against me...and he is not finished with me yet. John, my friend," Christian said, "I'm afraid we must part ways sooner than I expected."

"What? But...we only just—" John began.

156

"I know my friend, but we must. And John, I've got a great favor to ask of you." Christian got up from his place, took a seat closer to John, and whispered his request into his friend's ear. John was perplexed at first, but as he listened his expression grew solemn.

Finally John nodded in understanding. "I would be honored."

Christian placed his arm around John. "Thank you my friend." Then he turned to Watchful: "Have you got a sword?"

The porter pressed his lips together and bobbed his head slowly. "Yes. But as this is the last Palace before the Dark River you must surely partake in a service of preparation."

Christian was not typically a man of ceremony, but he finally believed that he had passed over too many opportunities for instruction and fellowship to refuse another, and so he agreed. Though panged by a biting sense of renewed grief over the loss of Faithful, Christian couldn't help but smile at the thought of what Faithful's reaction would be to Christian's participation in a Palace service—and what a Palace!

"What must I do?" Christian asked.

Watchful scowled and scratched his beard.

"Have you never been in an Evangelist Palace before now?"

Christian shook his head: "No...never."

"Well then," he said, pointing to a winding set of stairs nearby that descended to an unseen level. "At the foot of that stairway is a corridor, and at the end of it, a door. You will be told what to do when you arrive." Then Watchful looked at John. "It would be good for you to go with him."

John led the way down the hall shaped as an archway. The hall was straight and narrow, comprised of smoothed vanilla colored stone, and at its end was an unassuming arched door made of cedar. The lamps along the wall reflected off the door's surface, and it echoed back a wooden gold that brightened the atmosphere in the passageway with each step the pilgrims took.

Upon arriving, Christian and John saw that there was no latch for them to enter. They looked around for a solution to the riddle and found chiseled into the stone above the door, the following:

157

Christian smiled, remembering the inscription in the Wicket Gate at the beginning of his journey. He leaned forward and knocked. They waited for several seconds.

No response.

Then John knocked. They waited and watched the fire flicker in the lamps for several moments. The flames reminded Christian again of his family and the impending judgment from his actions that felt so certain to come upon them. A sense of urgency flowed through his blood and his heart began to pound. Faithful had entrusted his mother's salvation to Yeshua alone. Could Christian?

Just as Christian was raising his hand again to knock with a more earnest intent, the door opened and a clean-shaven young man with dark skin stood before them, dressed in a single white tunic that covered him completely from neck to foot.

"Welcome, my brothers," he said in a voice that was rich, warm, and confident. An open hand waved them into a small square vestibule constructed of stone and plaster. When John and Christian had entered, the man shut the door. Through an open archway leading to an adjacent chamber, Christian caught glimpses of two other men, of similar look and dress as their current host, walking about and lighting wall lamps. The young man before them continued. "Watchful, the porter of this Palace, has commended me to help prepare pilgrims such as you, which brings me great joy. The noble quests to which you are called by the King are perilous journeys fraught with danger on all sides, at all times. But don't be discouraged. Seek the King with all your heart, soul, mind, and strength, for He is always near."

The young man looked over his shoulder, then back at Christian and John. "My brothers have prepared the sanctuary; all is ready for us. Follow me."

Following the young man, the pilgrims moved into the chamber. It was spherical with a domed ceiling that curved some twenty feet above. The chamber had no windows or furniture and was large enough to comfortably contain at least fifty people. Remarkably, it appeared that the room had been hewn from a single great stone. The two men that Christian had seen moving about the room minutes before now stood silently against the wall at the perimeter of the chamber, and permeating the air was the pleasant fragrance of apples and cinnamon.

Their host moved away from them to the right and, with a wave of his hand, motioned Christian and John to stand side-by-side in an area near the center of the room. Before them, inserted into the stone floor, was a Cross of blackened wood taller than either man with a circle of thorny vines hanging at the top. A single scarlet robe, torn and frayed, was draped across the horizontal beam and a nail could be seen toward the bottom of the vertical beam, upon which hung the chords of a whip.

"See the Cross upon which Yeshua, the Son of El Shaddai, made His Atonement for all. Without this submission to the will of His Father the quests which you have agreed to accept would be wholly in vain. You are rebels and betrayers before the Judgment Seat of El Shaddai, justly condemned to eternal destruction for your actions against His Law. The Cross before you is rightly *your* Cross. The cruel punishment Yeshua suffered upon it is rightly *your* punishment. As it is written in the Book: 'He was pierced through for our transgressions, He was crushed for our iniquities; the chastening for our well-being fell upon Him, and by His scourging we are healed.' "

Christian's eyes were fixed on the Cross before him even as the words spoken cut him through his spirit. Not long ago, the weight upon his conscience was unbearable. Christian went hard to his knees, thankful for the atonement that had been paid for his wrongdoing. He began to think of all his actions against Yeshua on his campaigns for Apollyon—actions that he thought were saving his family but he now realized had only condemned him before El Shaddai. All his hopelessness, fear, despondency, and anger from the injustices which occurred in Vanity bubbled up through his throat, manifesting themselves in great aching sobs. During this outpouring of emotion, it occurred to him that with each heaving of his shoulders the remaining burden of his past diminished, until it was just a scar in his memory.

"Take heart my friends, and be at peace," the young man said. "By your faith it is declared unto you in Yeshua's Name: all your trespasses are forgiven you. El Shaddai has accepted the atonement of His Son for your sedition against Him. You have been made worthy to enter Celestial City because Yeshua, the Son of El Shaddai and True King of Creation, is worthy. He has clothed you with His righteousness. Guard this knowledge well against disbelief, for there are many who would take it from you in their doubt and arrogance, and many who would tempt you to rejoin them in their treason against El Shaddai. Yeshua is alive and coming again soon for judgment on

159

those who reject the grace and mercy of His Father through Himself, and for the re-creation of Heaven and Earth for all the saints of His family—for you are truly His children!"

The man indicated for his brethren to come forward and continued, "Receive this new raiment of the King as a sign that His Spirit is with you always." Christian turned and saw the two men holding between them a shimmering white, three-buttoned, patterned tunic of silk—a type fit for a high prince of a great land and just like the one he had seen John wearing. As the men moved forward to clothe Christian in the princely garment, they sang to Christian and John a beautiful passage from the Book, in a tone that started deep and built with a rumbling strength, filling the chamber:

For the death that He died,
He died to sin once for all;
But the life that He lives,
He lives to God (El Shaddai).
Even so consider yourselves
To be dead to sin,
But alive to God in Yeshua.
Therefore do not let sin
Reign in your mortal body
So that you obey its lusts,
And do not go on presenting
The members of your body to sin
As instruments of unrighteousness;
But present yourselves to God
As those alive from the dead,
And your members as instruments
Of righteousness to God.

Although Christian only saw the three men singing, the chamber echoes made it sound as if a whole choir were joining in.

After the singing ended, the lead man raised a hand, as if in greeting.

"The Spirit of the almighty and merciful Lord bless you and protect you," he concluded. "Go in His peace."

Christian and John bowed their heads briefly, and then exited the sanctuary the way they had come. Watchful met them at the end of the corridor archway. He directed John to the maidens of the Palace, who were waiting to show him things that would strengthen his heart, soul, and mind for the tasks that awaited him on the Road.

Christian was led by Watchful into the Palace armory, which was a low narrow chamber of polished white granite about fifty paces in length. Alcoves, lit by small slits open to the outside, lined both sides of the chamber and red-stained platforms, fashioned from the same stone as the chamber, were set in the alcoves upon which were all manner of artifacts, each with its own story and each ready to be wielded as needed.

"Here is the Rod of Moses," Watchful explained, "which was used in the service of El Shaddai to turn the great river of a defiant people into blood, in the parting of a great sea to save another, and to bring forth an unceasing spring of water from a rock to refresh that same people in the desert, when it had been commanded of Moses by El Shaddai."

The porter moved forward with purpose, past a few of the alcoves, to a mallet and twisted iron tent peg.

"In the days when El Shaddai worked through judges, this mallet and peg were used by the wife of a tent-dweller to slay an enemy of El Shaddai's people that the woman had cunningly wooed to sleep. Her husband was an ally of this man, but her trust was in El Shaddai and so she was used by Him to complete the victory He had already delivered to her people."

Next they moved to an alcove with high shelves full of broken pitchers, ram horns, and small torches. "These tokens are witnesses that El Shaddai delivers victory against His enemies despite all appearances. A great judge in the service of El Shaddai long ago defeated an army four hundred and fifty times greater than his own. With only clay pitchers, horns, and torches, El Shaddai gave this godless army into the hand of His judge and small force. The day is comin' when these horns'll sound again, these torches'll again be lit, and the immense armies of El Shaddai's enemies'll be routed before Him to their destruction."

161

Next, Christian was shown a platform with a cattle goad and the darkened jaw-bone of a donkey.

"These were used as weapons to incur severe casualties against the enemies of El Shaddai. They were employed by men of no great renown or pedigree before His callin'. Foolish is the one who presumes the Father of Yeshua can't make Himself a weapon of any material or design to destroy an enemy. What men consider weak, He makes strong, and He chooses instruments *He* deems best able to perform His purposes."

They had reached the last pair of alcoves, the first of which had upon its granite post a Sling and Stone while leaning beneath was a large, beautiful bronze sword.

"El Shaddai calls the most unlikely of us to achieve His greatest tasks. Here we see the sling of a shepherd boy an' the stone he used to defeat a monstrous giant. First, the boy declared the foe's defeat by the Word of El Shaddai, which the giant mocked, and then he brought the giant down with this small stone. To pronounce the victory of El Shaddai to all who witnessed the act, the boy cut off the enemy's head with his own sword, which you see lyin' against the column below. The boy grew to be a man of El Shaddai, one of His people's greatest leaders, and even now he waits in Celestial City for the Last Battle."

Watchful turned toward the last alcove, which contained a table with twelve blades of varying sizes and makes. Christian's eyes were fixed intently on the Giant's bronze sword as Watchful began to explain the others further along.

"These were the weapons of many rulers and captains who served El Shaddai well. They were granted gifts according to their prayers and trust: wisdom, strength, protection. Wherever these blades were stretched, El Shaddai scattered His enemies before their tips as a sign of His might, just wrath, and everlastin' covenant."

Christian finally turned his attention away from the Giant's sword back to Watchful, and the pair turned aside to another short corridor brilliantly lit by a circular painted window set into the wall. Just below the window was a tall block of the purest crystal-stone, flanked by two equally tall columns of similar fashion. Draped between the two pillars were pearlescent satin curtains of fine gold, glittering silver, and majestic purple. Suspended above the center column was a gleaming longsword of a length, weight, and presence that Christian was sure no mortal man could wield. Upon the pommel and crossguard was an intricate display of silver and gold of the rarest skill, the handle was wrapped in crimson leather and the blade and hilt seemed to have been burnished a hundred times a day to a mirrored finish.

"The Longblade of Yeshua, our Savior and King," the porter said with quiet reverence. "There are none, for which this just weapon is meant, who will escape its double-sharp reach. It'll defeat the demon-princes and their servants with merciless ferocity. It'll cut down in a breath any man whom they've raised up as the champion of their deceptive and blasphemous rebellion, which has brought lawlessness. It is the weapon of the victory already won for us by Yeshua's death, His resurrection, and His ascension."

Christian stood there, bathing in its glow, and he longed for the day in which he could follow into battle the Hand that raised that wonderful blade on that day.

Watchful grasped the pilgrim's shoulder.

"And it'll empty out the vengeance of El Shaddai upon all those who have martyred His children."

Christian snapped his head to his host, but said nothing.

"Yes, John told me about Faithful."

Christian struggled to speak, but finally found his voice. "I miss him."

"Leave the execution of justice to El Shaddai," Watchful instructed.

"I'm in no position to judge my friend's murderers," Christian replied. "I have enough blood of the Evangelists on my own hands."

Watchful nodded but remained silent for a moment. "Faithful is with our Lord in Celestial City now. Come."

The porter led Christian down another short corridor and into a small ante-chamber. At its center was a raised pedestal to which Watchful directed Christian to stand. Against each of three walls was an empty table of cedar, and filling each of the three walls was a large pane of colored glass: one depicted a great radiant eye upon a horizon, peering through a triangle above a beautiful landscape; another illustrated a wounded lamb carrying a white banner with a scarlet cross upon it, marching triumphantly past a row of wheat and grape vines enclosed in a triangle; the third was of a dove emerging from a triangle and descending through a sky glowing with fiery hues, as if the earth it was approaching was lit by a thousand flames. The mid-morning sun brought vivid life to these colors so that it almost seemed as though Christian was looking through portals at live scenes.

The four maidens of the Palace, with John behind, entered the small chamber with sober expressions. Three of the maidens—Charity, Prudence, and Discretion—brought pieces of burnished armor and chainmail, while Piety carried a heavy cloth mantle the pale brown shade of sea shells. The armor and chainmail, which carried the marks of use despite its polished luster, were placed upon the three tables. The cloth garment was taken by Charity and Piety and unfolded between them: a knee-length sleeveless wool robe. Adorned on its front was a large scarlet cross, trimmed in gold, which stretched across the chest and from neck to waist. Each arm of the Cross had the base appearance of four flat-headed nails tapering at the center.

Watchful picked up the coat of mail and proceeded to place it upon Christian. As the porter fastened the protective layer upon his torso, the women began to sing a new hymn, and Watchful joined in:

Praise to the Lord, the Almighty,
The King of Creation!
Oh my soul, praise Him,
For He is your health and salvation!
All you who hear,
Now to His temple draw near;
Praise Him in glad adoration.

The hymn continued as Charity and Prudence stepped forward to place the robe upon Christian.

Praise to the Lord, Who when darkness
Of sin is abounding!
When godless men triumph,
All virtue confounding,
He shines His light,
Chasing the horrors of night,

164

Saints with His mercy surrounding!

The chant thankfully continued, because Christian had not tired of the voices and found immense strength in the words.

Piety retreated from the chamber, motioning John to come with her. Meanwhile Watchful and the other maidens placed the pieces of armor upon Christian: laminar pauldrons for his shoulders and upper arms leather-strapped to a thin strip of metal that covered the area just below his neck, and steel vambraces that covered his fore-arms and wrist. They sang on:

Praise to the Lord, O let all that is in me
Adore Him!
All that has life and breath,
Come now with praises before Him.
Let the Amen
Sound from His people again,
Gladly for we do adore Him.

Piety and John returned as Christian was making the final adjustments to his new armor. Piety carried the weathered and faded crimson cloak that had been given to Christian by his friend Interpreter in ages past—at least it seemed so long ago. The cloak had been lovingly cleaned and mended as best it could.

John held a triangular shield and close-fitting helmet. The shield was etched with the design of a lamb, in the same crimson shade as the cross on his robe and very similar in appearance to that of the wounded lamb upon the pane of stained glass. The helmet was smooth and fierce and it covered the whole head, except for the eyes, mouth, and chin. Intricately hammered scrollwork swirled across all the metal, often splitting off and curling at the ends.

Now fitted with his suit of protection, Watchful smiled with satisfaction.

"Magnificent, my friend," Watchful bellowed. "Now you're ready for the course you've chosen to embark upon, and upon which El Shaddai will bestow His blessing. But first…you must choose a weapon!"

CHAPTER EIGHTEEN

The crisp wind carried a faint scream to Christian and John's ears. High and strong upon its hillock, Palace Beautiful loomed behind the men in the rays of the afternoon sun, achingly magnificent among the scores of trees adorned in autumn's splendor. Christian shifted the pack of supplies strung across his back, while John grasped tighter hold of a walking stick that rose past his head.

Christian looked into the eastern distance to where the Road met the horizon, and he discerned wisps of smoke rising and blown about. Ahead the land was barren and rocky, and the rare tree was skeletal and pathetic.

And all was too quiet.

"Christian, please, you mustn't," John pleaded to the warrior who kept his face set on the Narrow Road ahead.

"There is no other way."

The silence that persisted finally turned Christian's eyes from the desolate landscape to his companion.

"Don't worry, my friend. I no longer fear death, for it will not be my end. I have chosen rightly this time. Our King has already conquered the grave."

Christian looked down at the Book in his hands, and then extended the leather-bound treasure to John. "Take care of this for me and my family, for faith in this world is reality in Celestial City."

John nodded and carefully took the Book as tears began to form in the corners of his eyes. "Your sacrifice will be a beacon for others, as your dear friend's was for us."

"Yeshua's sacrifice is the one to remember above all," Christian replied. "It is He who grants us the strength to offer our lives for our neighbors. It is He who graciously uses our works to work His loving will. Without His Spirit in us we could do nothing, and without His love we would have and be nothing."

166

Christian locked arms with John, who pulled him into a quick embrace. Then Christian again continued on his journey, alone. His friend watched him until the knight was out of his sight, and then John commenced his great task for Christian in the opposite direction.

* * *

Christian watched the last sliver of the sun disappear beneath the horizon as he wiped a drop of water from his lips. A little farther along the path, on the other side of a nearby hill, Christian saw firelight rising in the darkening sky and more smoke could also be seen rising into the sky as it reflected the firelight. Suppressing a chill, Christian continued down the Road and up the peak.

At the summit, Christian beheld a grizzly sight: at the foot of the slope on both sides of the Road lay the fiery ruins of a merchant caravan. Directly on the Road, among blackened and scattered bodies of men and beasts and the debris of covered wagons and trading supplies, Christian saw the back of a tall wisp of a man sitting on a fallen, bloating corpse of a horse. The man's ashen, gaunt arms protruded from the iron suit that encased his torso.

Apollyon, Lord of all Demons.

Christian placed his supply pack on the ground and moved toward his great foe with deliberate strides. He was still dozens of paces away when Apollyon turned his head.

Christian halted, unsure of whether or not the demon-prince was taking stock of him.

Apollyon tossed his snack—a gnawed human hand!—and sighed with exasperation bordering on boredom.

"Where did you come from, friend?" he hissed slowly. "And where are you going?"

"Sorry," Christian said as he slowly proceeded forward, "I was held up a bit after killing your minions."

Suddenly, with superhuman speed, Apollyon was facing Christian but made no forward movement. It looked as though the body that Apollyon possessed had once

167

belonged to a handsome man but, now void of El Shaddai's breath of life, Apollyon was unable to keep the body from decaying.

The hair on Apollyon's head was so thin that his pallid scalp could be seen through its dark patches. His eyes were small, dark, and oddly reflective of the abysmal scene that surrounded them. His skin seemed almost too small for his strong but gangly frame.

Apollyon chuckled, although it was more like several short hisses. "This world belongs to me. I'm the god of it!" he shouted, losing control. He then regained his calm demeanor as quickly as he had lost it and asked, as though he were hurt, "Why have you run from your lord?"

Christian surveyed the scene of butchery around him, discerning the distinct robed attire of citizens that would have lived in Vanity.

"These were your own servants?" Christian exclaimed in disgust.

Apollyon shrugged "So it would appear. And they served my appetite well."

Christian swallowed down the unsettling in his stomach. "You're growing desperate, beast! Since when do you do your own hunting?"

Apollyon bent his head and studied Christian.

"You're losing," the knight added.

"Losing what?"

"You're having trouble finding enough servants to feed you, and you think that I can help you recruit."

Apollyon shrugged again. "Once a traitor, always a traitor. But you served me well, once. The other humans follow you…you're a *hero*," he mocked.

"That was different. I once wanted the freedom to rule myself. Now I serve the True King."

Apollyon hissed and spat, and the invoking of a reference to Yeshua won Christian a low animalistic growl from the demon lord.

Apollyon immediately changed his tone to feign innocent curiosity, and he gestured toward a charred woman protecting an equally-charred child. "Why is it that humans always protect their young?" he asked, revealing fanged teeth.

"You will not touch my family!"

"What makes you think I do not have them here, to show you the tortured end of each of them in turn?"

Christian was not fooled, "If you had my family, you would show them to me now. They have evaded your grasp."

Apollyon remained stoic. "You were my child once..." Apollyon squinted his eyes even smaller, as if peering into Christian's soul. "What will it take to bring you back? Money? Power?"

"You have nothing that I want."

Apollyon continued to gaze at Christian. "You're wrong you know. I'm not having trouble finding servants." The demon-prince leapt off the carcass and stood before Christian with unearthly speed. Christian staggered backward to put some distance between himself and his foe. "I have more than ever before. I simply desire *more*."

"You *are* building an army..."

"It'll be a shame to lose a smart one like you," Apollyon again mocked, sarcastically. "Then again, how rational can you be? Do you know what you'll face if you continue on this journey? Your course is dangerous. Lots of suffering...fear...the unknown. The One you have chosen to follow doesn't much care for rebels and dissidents...like *us*."

"I have not chosen Him, but He has chosen me and marked me as His own. Because I am His, I know that death is only the doorway to everlasting life."

Apollyon studied Christian for a long moment and Christian believed that he could discern a hint of envious rage, though Apollyon did his best to hide it. "I hope that your family will be as fortunate."

His family had been threatened for the last time! Christian charged at his enemy with ferocity as he moved to draw his sword, but dark clouds of smoke engulfed them, apparently conjured by Apollyon, making it difficult for Christian to see or breathe and he postponed his attack until he could find clean air to take a breath.

Apollyon's eyes glowed with rage as he sprung through the air to meet Christian. There was still no time to draw his weapon from its sheath, so the knight hit Apollyon with his shield, causing the demon to spit fiery napalm on the ground. Christian recoiled, then dropped to his knees and rolled, finally drawing the bronze sword that

had once belonged to Goliath the Giant, then King David, just as Apollyon leapt at him again.

Christian swung his blade again and again, but Apollyon deflected each slash with his bare, taloned hands.

Fortunately, Christian had learned from his previous encounter with Belial and he now had a weapon far superior to the demon-fashioned blade he wielded in that battle. As a result, the demon-prince gave up a little ground with each attack.

Christian spotted an advantage just off the Road, and through a series of feints and thrusts he managed to drive the gaunt demon into a deep pit. Apollyon screeched as he fell and Christian peered into the pit but lost sight of his arch-enemy.

Suddenly, a monstrous hiss erupted out of the abyss and Christian saw a black fire-and-smoke shape climbing rapidly toward him. Christian leapt back, narrowly avoiding a decapitating bite as a fire-and-smoke serpent burst past him into the night sky. Once high in the sky above Christian, the beast turned and descended, building momentum and breathing flame. Christian jumped out of the way just in time to avoid his demise, but he still suffered painful burns on both hands and legs.

The knight turned as the smoky serpent landed in a coiled heap of smoke and then slithered toward him with the silent movement of billowing smoke upon the scorched earth.

Christian swiped at the serpent with his sword, but the blade only moved through the black smoke. The monster hissed—almost a bestial laugh—and spit more flame at its prey like a cobra spitting venom. Christian leapt past the flame and bounded into the smoke, screaming through the blasts of heat toward where he thought the center of the beast might be found. He stayed close to the ground and finally caught a glimpse of a thin figure at the serpent's core. He couldn't hesitate: Christian charged at Apollyon's human form, thrashed his sword wildly, and made contact. A shriek erupted through the air, followed by a hiss, and the knight found himself being knocked backward as the serpent pulled back into a defensive coil. Christian's head slammed onto the ground, sending his helmet flying. He dropped his sword, which was red with heat, and lay stunned and bleeding from the ears. His breathing was labored and, in a daze, Christian groped in desperate futility for his sword.

Meanwhile, the black serpent dissipated once more into lifeless smoke, blowing away with the next breeze. The man-form of Apollyon glided quickly through the dissipating smoke toward Christian, and when he was close Apollyon stopped for a moment to take in his work. He then pounced, pinning Christian to the ground.

Apollyon beat Christian with incredible force and hatred. He stopped only to grasp Christian's neck with one taloned hand and raise the other for a fatal slash. "I wonder if your children will taste more like you...or their mother."

With a desperate cry, Christian moved enough to grope just a little farther for the sword that had once slain another great enemy of El Shaddai, and by His grace the knight gripped the handle.

Sword in hand, Christian thrust its blade between a seam in Apollyon's Crest within his nightmarish breastplate and deep into the ribs of his stolen flesh. Apollyon lurched back and words from the Book came to Christian's weak lips: "Do not rejoice over me, O my enemy...though I fall, I will *rise again*...the Lord is my Light!"

The demon-prince opened his mouth wide in frustrated rage. And Christian pushed the sword through each eye causing a hideous scream each time. The distinctive steel breastplate of Apollyon dissolved into smoke and the human carcass he had occupied relaxed as Apollyon's smoky spirit-form drained away in streams of black smoke, leaving a lifeless, defeated corpse crumpling to the ground.

Then Christian was alone.

As he felt his life seeping out of him, the courageous pilgrim muttered one last prayer: "Thank you, Lord, for this victory."

CHAPTER NINETEEN

Christian moaned in pain.

He had presumably slept all night in the chilly autumn air, with only the heat from nearby smoldering carcasses and debris to keep him from chilling to the bone. His spent body had grown stiff and sore during his prolonged unconsciousness.

The new day was dreary with a chilling grey mist. Christian mustered all of his strength to roll onto his stomach, with more groaning, and continued his journey at a crawl, leaving all but his clothes and armor behind. When this proved cumbersome, he removed the heavily damaged armor and was finally able to stagger to his feet thanks to his lightened load, and thus the pilgrim was able to trudge forward.

The rocky terrain became grasslands, where the sun finally emerged to gladden his spirit. The grasslands soon gave way to stunning mountain landscapes painted in all the many colors of peak autumn. The Narrow Road led Christian through this idyllic setting down into a valley, where he could soon hear the sound of rushing water.

Christian continued to stumble along the Narrow Road, which was now a true paved road with stone walls along either side, when a small bend in the path brought him face-to-face with a lion. The pilgrim was so weak that his surprise at the animal caused him to fall.

"Not again..." he mumbled. But the lion just stood beside the path, watching him curiously. A small white lamb jumped across the Road, at which the lion took notice but did little else, and Christian gaped at the sight in awe.

"I am sorry if he frightened you," came a voice. "You have no need to fear. Might I assume that you are looking for Celestial City?"

Christian looked up toward the voice. A winged Celestial Being was approaching, shining as though a hundred suns shone at his back. When he arrived, he graciously helped the pilgrim to his feet. Immediately Christian felt a portion of his strength return, even as he struggled with the reality of the question. Had he really made it?

"Yes, I am," he answered.

The being smiled and motioned toward the east. "This way."

"Sir, am I close?"

The being nodded, half-turned his face to Christian, and smiled. "Very."

After a few minutes, a wide and rapidly-flowing river rushed across the Narrow Road.

Christian looked at the being and anxiety arose quickly into his heart. "Is this the only way?"

"For you, yes."

The Celestial being and the pilgrim moved closer to the perilous trial that raged within the riverbanks.

"What is this?" Christian asked.

"Some call it the Dark River. It is the last obstacle on your journey to the King's Country. Those with faith in Yeshua have nothing to fear."

Grasping the arm of the glowing figure, Christian placed one booted foot into the rapids, and then the other. The frigid water quickly engulfed him to the thigh. He turned to the Celestial Being, who removed his arm from beneath the pilgrim's hand.

"The City is just across the river," the figure reminded him. "Keep its light in your eyes and focus on the song you hear."

Christian looked across to the other side as he moved forward a bit further but he saw nothing but rolling, treeless hills. "I see no city. I hear no song."

"You will."

When Christian was waist-deep in the water, he tried with great difficulty to remain still and upright. He closed his eyes, took a deep breath, and calmed himself. With new resolve, he waded into the deeper, more turbulent waters. Further still, he found that he could no longer keep his head above water. He fought against the rushing and swirling torrent with all his might, but his fighting ceased as his strength dwindled. The current pulled Christian beneath the surface and into darkening depths. Fully submerged, the pilgrim was at the mercy of the frigid river, powerless against its violent undercurrent. The setting grew dark as pitch, and Christian felt nothing of his body. He felt so light, he believed he should float back to the surface.

Finally, Christian realized that he had died.

Yet Christian was still conscious, and vulnerable. Memories assaulted him like a flurry of blows to his head and stomach: allowing Apollyon to goad him into a battle; his failure to enact an escape from Vanity with his friend; his focus on following the Road primarily to help his family even after Yeshua had rebuked him for it; his choice to take the lives of innocents for the demon-princes in order to spare those of his wife and children; the rejection of the fellowship and instruction offered by Faithful and the Palaces—egregious errors, all of them. Christian realized this trial was meant to bring the pilgrim face-to-face with his rebellion and utter depravity. He was not worthy of life in Celestial City.

Christian needed help...help from Yeshua, his King who had paid his ransom price. If only he could cling to the hem of His robe or once more hear Him proclaim the sweetness of His mercy.

Just then a beam of light penetrated the water and Christian could hear beautiful music, as if a great tune were being played by more instruments than Christian could fathom.

He felt a tug and the light seemed to be getting rapidly closer. The pilgrim moved his head sluggishly toward where he believed he felt a grip. Indeed, there was a hand grasping his robe, which was now white as snow. Christian noticed that his rescuer's hand was scarred with an elongated hole through the wrist. Grasping the hand, Christian was pulled out of the now-calm river and held fast until his feet found sand beneath them. As he stepped ashore he took further notice of his appearance. In addition to his clothing, which was now a brilliant white, Christian found that his wounds were not only healed but that his skin was cleaner than he could ever remember. He stopped to bask in the constant light of El Shaddai that touched all of his surroundings.

The beach line quickly merged to become a small grassy hill, which rolled down to a wide valley. Nearby was a long mason-work bridge, edged by short walls full of intricate designs, which disappeared into hedgerows as it descended gently: the continuation of the Narrow Road.

Where there had previously appeared to be nothing but an open field to veiled eyes now stood a massive, jasper-walled Capital. Immense pearlescent gates were open wide and on all sides climbed high, light-brushed emerald slopes of lush mountains. The City was situated upon a still river of the clearest aqua-beryl, which flowed around and under the city walls. Celestial City spiraled upward with Mount Zion, around which the city was built, as much as it did out and back out of sight, the size and arrangement of ten thousand Palace Beautifuls in all dimensions.

Crowds of glorified humans and angelic beings stood on the ramparts like lit candles and countless others flowed nearly indistinguishable on paths among innumerable garden courtyards and golden-bright structures topped by spires of all makes or tiled by iris sapphire. Tall windows of pure crystal and cream topaz churned with the interior glow of warm fire-light. The fragrance of sweet spices permeated the air and unending songs of victory and honor emanated from the City. From somewhere ahead radiated an Almighty Light, another Light shone from the sky directly above, and one other Light from much closer on one side.

Christian's vision settled on the Light that shown so completely upon his face. He went to his knees before the dazzling figure of Yeshua, dressed in the same hooded lambskin coat of many colors that Christian had seen in his previous encounter. Christian took the hem of this garment to his lips over and over, tears spilling from his eyes and onto the feet of his Savior.

"Well done, My good and faithful servant," He said. "You kept My command and followed Me."

Christian stayed prostrate. "My Lord, I have come to join Your army. I must beg of you to gather your Men of Arms so that we may retake Your lands before my family...before they..."

"You may return with Me, Christian. The time is near, but the family gifted to you is no longer your concern. They were always Mine."

"My Lord, of course they are! I mean...I want them to be here, with us. I can't fail them! Apollyon is building an army."

"Apollyon and his servants rightly fear Me." Yeshua paused for a moment before continuing. "Lives laid down for one's neighbor in faith and love are most certainly seen by El Shaddai." Yeshua reached down a hand and pulled Christian to his feet, locking His eyes on His beloved child with deep sincerity. "It is a difficult task that you asked of your new companion, to walk back along the Road. But as he has undertaken the journey in love for you, his brother, I shall bless his labor and work his suffering for My good. This as a witness to the grace of the Father. It is not His will that any should perish, even though it is difficult to walk the Narrow Road, much less find it. Trust Me, Christian."

"Yes, my Lord." Christian had pleaded his case to the One who had loved the most. From then and onward he would leave the matter with his King.

"Faithful's father felt much the same as you do now," Yeshua added and turned his gaze. "My sheep hear My voice and they follow Me."

Christian turned to see what Yeshua was looking at as a familiar voice called his name.

"Christian!"

Christian looked toward the bridge. Walking briskly toward him was a man wearing the mantle of eternal life to its full extent. Within a few strides he was embracing Faithful as tightly as if he were his own brother.

When they separated, Faithful led Christian to the two men who had accompanied him to this welcoming. Christian embraced with both hands the arm of the Evangelist who had warned him to flee from the wrath to come, and then embraced another dear friend: Faithful's father.

The four friends turned to look at the City again and recounted their journeys. Then Christian looked over his shoulder at Yeshua, who nodded His confirmation: it was time. The four men moved onto the bridge: four pilgrims progressing to the City they had been given by their King.

THE
ARRIVAL.

EPILOGUE

BANG-BANG-BANG!!!

Christy sat up with a terrible start, gasping from the realness of the images—an experience so real, except under the similitude of a dream. She quickly found Matthew and Joseph lying with her, while Sammie shared a bed with Deedee on the other side of the sleeping loft in the Interpreter's small house.

BANG-BANG-BANG-BANG-BANG-BANG-BANG!!!

The front door.

Christy pushed out of bed, threw on the robe that hung on the nearby railing as she descended the small ladder with the same motion. It was much harder to tie the robe with shaking hands, but she managed it. Then she was wiping the moisture from her face with the other hand. She was hardly in a worse state to entertain a persistent guest.

Where was their host?

Christy crossed the main living space to the door and threw it open without hesitation. The light of daybreak flooded around a thin, clean-shaven face attached to a scarecrow's body. The man was covered in a dark brown woolen cloak and held a tall staff. Tucked in his belt was an unmarked bound Manuscript. An aura emanated from him that kept her speechless.

"Christy?" he said immediately. There was great urgency in his tone.

"Yes..."

"I have been sent to help guide you along the Narrow Road to the safety of the True King's City where your husband awaits. Wake your children—for we must flee! Flee from the wrath to come!"

The Narrow Road

If you enjoyed this story and would like to see The Narrow Road
on the big screen, please visit:

www.narrowroadmovie.com/get-involved

www.ingramcontent.com/pod-product-compliance
Lightning Source LLC
Chambersburg PA
CBHW050735250626
47155CB00005B/1786